Fiction

Table Number Seven

BOOKS BY

VICTOR CANNING

Mr Finchley Discovers His England
Mr Finchley Goes to Paris
Mr Finchley Takes the Road
Polycarp's Progress
Fly Away Paul
Matthew Silverman
Fountain Inn
Everyman's England (travel)
Green Battlefield
Panther's Moon
The Chasm
The Golden Salamander
A Forest of Eyes
The House of the Seven Flies
Venetian Bird
The Man from the "Turkish Slave"
Castle Minerva
His Bones are Coral
The Hidden Face
The Manasco Road
The Dragon Tree
Young Man on a Bicycle (and other stories)
The Burning Eye
A Delivery of Furies
Black Flamingo
Delay on Turtle (and other stories)
The Limbo Line
The Scorpio Letters
The Whip Hand
Doubled in Diamonds
The Python Project
The Melting Man
Queen's Pawn
The Great Affair
Firecrest
The Rainbird Pattern
The Finger of Saturn
The Mask of Memory
The Kingsford Mark
The Doomsday Carrier
Birdcage
The Satan Sampler
Fall from Grace
The Boy on Platform One
Vanishing Point
Raven's Wind
Birds of a Feather
Table Number Seven

Smiler: a trilogy
The Runaways
Flights of the Grey Goose
The Painted Tent

The Arthurian trilogy
The Crimson Chalice
The Circle of the Gods
The Immortal Wound

Table Number Seven

VICTOR CANNING

HEINEMANN : LONDON

William Heinemann Ltd
Michelin House, 81 Fulham Road, London SW3 6RB

LONDON MELBOURNE AUCKLAND

First published 1987
© Estate of Victor Canning 1987

Reprinted 1988

Canning, Victor
   Table number seven.
   I. Title
   823'.912[F]   PR6005.A486
   ISBN 0–434–10749–2

FIC

Filmset by Deltatype, Ellesmere Port
Printed in Great Britain by
Billing & Sons Ltd, Worcester

This book is dedicated
to Victor Canning's readers

ONE

ON THE ROUND table in the centre of the waiting room there were four neatly arranged piles of magazines spaced around a tall vase full of dried leaves and several spikes of purple headed teasels. They looked nice, Lily thought – but, more than that, they would last a long time. She supposed that this had been in the mind of whoever had been responsible for the arrangement. One of the girls who worked in the office, she supposed. Everything was spick and span, neat and tidy. She put back the copy of a woman's magazine she had idly leafed through . . . not really having registered much of what she had seen. Her mind was too full of a reasonable curiosity which had been with her for the last two days . . . from the time when she had received the letter asking her to call – the day and the time precisely given, and it would be presumed that these would be convenient to her unless she telephoned . . . and so on. Well . . . it was convenient and here she was – Mr Tredwell at the shop, good-natured and easy-going as usual, having made no bones about giving her time off and saying with a big grin, "If it's to tell you you've been left a fortune we'll get married, sell up here and go and live happily ever after on the Costa Brava. How about that?"

Liking him, knowing by now his jokey ways she had grinned and said, "No, thanks. You'd just keep me working on here as a wife and without wages."

"Well, it had crossed my mind."

"Then uncross it . . ."

She smiled to herself. A nice man, widower, but with no

1

intention of ever remarrying. He was too comfortable the way he was. And as for herself . . . Well, love and marriage played little part in her daydreams. One day, she supposed, someone would come along who would see something in her which so far no one had ever seen. Plain Jane. That was her. But if no one did come along . . . well, there were plenty of women in the same boat. And on the other side, too, she supposed: plenty of men in the same fix.

At the moment, however, she was far from being at all concerned about love and marriage. There was – even though she disapproved of it – an edge of excitement and slightly unworthy curiosity in her about what the solicitor was going to tell her. She had enough wit to know that it must have something to do with Mrs Ellington, lately deceased, for whom, two evenings a week for the last five years, she had gone in to her flat, made a dinner for her which they had both shared and then afterwards had read to her for an hour from one or other of her favourite books. Some she had read so often that she could almost – it seemed now – do it from memory. Not that she could, of course – but that was the way it seemed. But more than that was her almost mania for the language of flowers. Every night after the reading and before the twice-weekly supper they shared there had been the cross-examination of the language of flowers, a selection right through from Abatina for fickleness to Zinnia for thoughts of absent friends. The quiz was a mania for her.

And then, only a few weeks ago, she had gone into the flat without knocking or ringing as she always did and found the old dear sitting in her armchair, her head lolled to one side, her eyes closed and her mouth still smiling as though she had passed away with some warm enchanting thought . . . the language of flowers book on her lap and still held open by the thumb of her right hand just touching the entry . . . *Flowering reed . . . Confidence in Heaven.* And that was surely where she had gone. Of this Lily Franklin was sure.

Through the half-glazed inner wall of the waiting-room

2

she could see the blurred movement of people in the outer reception hall: neat and tidy and seeming briskly and importantly efficient young men and women.

The door of the waiting-room opened and one of the girl clerks held it back, smiled at her and said, "Miss Franklin. . . ? Mr Porter will see you. This way . . ."

She held the door for Lily and then went ahead of her down the corridor and opened, a heavy, half-glazed door, held it and motioned Lily to enter as she announced, "Miss Franklin . . . Mr Porter . . ."

A large, broad-shouldered man in a black jacket and pin-striped trousers, a tight-budded pink rose in the lapel of his jacket, rose from the chair behind his desk, gave her a big smile and waved to the empty chair in front of his desk, saying, "Miss Franklin. . . . Nice to see you. Do sit down, please."

"Thank you Mr Porter."

She sat down, settled herself comfortably, and noticed on one side of his desk a framed photograph of a woman standing on a lawn, an herbaceous border and a yew hedge behind her, and with a small boy pressed close to her side and held there by the woman's right arm. Mother and son, she thought: and even from here she could see in the boy's young face some shadow, some dim resemblance to the bland, composed face of the man sitting at his desk and smiling at her.

Mr Porter said, "For how many years did you know Mrs Ellington?"

"Oh, seven or eight, I think . . . I went first to do a little cleaning and some laundry work for her . . . and then, well, in a way we got to be friendly. I still worked for her – but it was all a bit different. More companionlike. She was a nice lady – but not without temper if you gave her cause."

He smiled. "I know that well. But she was never lacking in generosity?"

"Oh, no. But it weren't never no good asking for anything

3

. . . like some did. She had a mind of her own and didn't need anyone's help to make it up."

"You used to go in often and look after her . . . do her bits of shopping and other things?"

"Oh, yes. And read to her." She smiled. "Oh, dear, that was terrible at first . . . since I was no scholar and a lot of words came strange to me. But I got better at it in the end. I played for her, too, on the piano. Just any old bits and pieces of things I knew she liked. Not that I'm any big shakes . . . it was all mostly by ear and probably not very good. But she liked it. Mind you, you could never quite tell where you were with her. Not nothing bitchy, I don't mean. But odd. Like she'd say sometimes – *I'm going to make tomorrow a banana day . . . or a tomato day.* And so she would, eating nothing else." She paused for a moment or two, and then as he said nothing she went on, "I'm sorry . . . I run on sometimes."

"That's all right." Mr Porter looked at her in silence for a while, one hand rubbing his chin, the other playing a gentle five-fingered exercise on the red morocco leather of his desk top. Then he said, "Have you any idea why I've asked you to come in here today?"

She smiled. "Oh, yes. Because she was a lady what always kept her word."

"Perhaps you could explain that more fully?"

"Well, like you know, I'm sure. She knew what was going to happen to her, poor dear. Not that she snivelled about it – or even went the other way and got all . . . well, pious and churchy. No, she used to say 'swings and roundabouts and God knows best'. But she did ask me some while ago that when she went what would I like that she had. You know, to keep as a remembrance."

"Yes. And what did you say?"

"Well, it wasn't much really. Just a thin little old book she had. It was all about the language of flowers and what it meant . . . like bluebells for constancy and London pride for frivolity. Lovely the little paintings were. I said I'd like it.

Just a thin little thing with a painting of pansies on the cover. Do you know what pansies stand for, Mr Porter?"

He smiled, shook his head and said, "I have no idea."

"Thoughts. Good thoughts."

He shook his head indulgently, and laughed gently.

"Did you used to talk to Mrs Ellington like this?"

"Oh, yes. She liked a good gossip . . . or a chatter about out of the way things. Mind you, she knew about things that . . . well, were far out of my reach. She had visions sometimes. She'd tell me about them. Lovely ones . . . Just listening to her I'd get carried right away. She had a thing, too, which –"

She broke off, brief discomfort showing on her face and in her body stance.

"What kind of thing, Miss Franklin?"

"Well, she used to say – not to everyone of course . . . Oh no. It was something she kept very quiet about. Naturally, knowing what people might say. That she was scatty. But to the right people she was quite open about it."

"About what, Miss Franklin?"

"Why – that Jesus Christ often came back to earth. You know . . . like every ten or so years. Just to run his eye over things and see how they were going. It was no good arguing with her – and I never did, though others did. No, I never did – because in a way I didn't see why it couldn't happen. She often used to talk to me about it."

"She was really serious?"

"Oh, yes, sir, Mr Porter. She said she'd seen Him herself two or three times."

Mr Porter smiled. "Well, how very interesting." He was silent for a moment or two, his eyes fixed on her and then he said, "About the flower book – you are quite right. It will be given to you when you leave here. But she also left you something else."

"Yes, sir?"

"First of all, she has left you five thousand pounds and –"

"Five thousand what?"

5

"Pounds —"

"But I've never had . . . but she didn't have to do that. I mean she paid me well. There was no cause to —"

"Miss Franklin, Mrs Ellington was sound of mind and had a perfect right to leave her money in any legal and responsible way she chose. You get five thousand pounds — but on one condition. You and any friend you care to take with you — not a male friend — are at her expense to go on a Mediterranean cruise."

"Oh, how lovely. But I can't do that. Auntie Rachel hates the sea."

"That is not relevant. Her will explicitly states that the friend must in no way be related to you." He smiled suddenly and she noticed that he had one gold tooth in the far left of the top row of teeth. "Auntie will be looked after, I assure you. It was Mrs Ellington's wish that you go with someone of your own sex and generation."

"But she won't like it, sir."

"I think you will find she will. A member of my staff is with her now explaining everything. I am sure you will find all will be well. Mrs Ellington, old though she was, was a good organizer."

"She knew her own mind, sir. I know that. But all this . . . well, it's like her, of course. Good and generous — but also so unexpected. Spoke her mind to one and all if she saw the need . . . and she'd stand up to anybody to see right done . . . young or old, big or little. In a way she was a saint. She did more good than anyone could guess. I know, because I sometimes saw bits of it. And, what's more —" She broke off and then added, "I'm sorry, sir. But it's all a bit much and I'm . . . I'm . . . well, I don't know what I am."

Mr Porter smiled and standing up said, "I think I know very well what you are — and so did Mrs Ellington. Now what I suggest you do is to go quietly home, tell your aunt all about it — though you'll find she knows a little already — and then when you've arranged for someone to go with you just let me know and this office will make all the arrangements.

6

That's how Mrs Ellington wanted it to be. As you go out my secretary will give you some Mediterranean cruise brochures which you can take away and keep. Look them through and choose something which takes your fancy. And please –" he gave a long, low chuckle, "– don't look so upset and glum about things. I know it's a bit of a shock – but it's a nice one. You smiled as you came in here and said *Good morning*. Smile now."

Suddenly Lily laughed and shaking her head said, "Oh dear – that Mrs Ellington. Springing this on me." Then the joy going from her face, her look serious and concerned, she went on, "She shouldn't have done it . . . shouldn't have done it. I didn't do anything more for her than anyone would have done. I really didn't, sir."

*   *   *   *

She got off the bus at the corner of the road in which she lived with her aunt and, as she usually did – in a gesture which now in an innocent but superstitious way had become a habit with her – she raised her eyes to the long tree-green run of the hills up which the main road climbed on its way to Cirencester . . . to the long straight upland road along which the Roman cohorts had marched thousands of years before to see for the first time the silver snaking loops of the Severn river and, beyond, the green sweep of the Welsh hills. She liked reading about historical times . . . not just historical only books, but romances . . . gallant knights and damsels in distress and wandering minstrels and villains and villainesses triumphant until the last chapter and then . . . well, and then the cowled friar threw off his dusty brown habit and became a knight in shining armour with the great red cross of the Crusaders bold across his chest. Lovely . . . always a surprise though she knew it was coming. And now this – but this time really a surprise since Mrs Ellington had never given her any hint of what must have been in her mind for a long time. Poor dear . . . she had never complained much or given away how much she suffered, growing thinner and more haggard but always a smile of greeting and more ready to laugh than to complain.

When she turned into the garden gateway of the little green lawn that fronted her aunt's cottage it was to find Auntie Rachel, gloved and aproned, squatting on her kneeling mat weeding the long flowerbed under the front windows of Green Willows, 34 Hill View Terrace, Cheltenham (and neither herself nor her aunt minding that there was no true view of the rising hill except from the attic window; the attic itself seldom visited unless they wanted to store bits and pieces and things that might come in handy and empty suitcases and too good to throw away cardboard cases).

Aunt Rachel looked at her over her shoulder, smiled and then began to rise stiffly to her feet, taking for assistance the hand which Lily held out to her. She was a small, perky little woman, robin-jaunty and neat even when she did dirty work, more active than many other women of her age . . . fierce in her dislikes and disapprovals, putty in the hands of those she loved and tears ever prompt with genuine sadness at tragedy. . . . She took off her gardening gloves, came stiffly up off her knees, brushed a wisp of grey hair from one eye then smiled, overdoing it because, for comfort, she had, when she felt safe from visiting company, taken out her false teeth, and then said, "You got nothing to tell me. I dreamt it all last night – but didn't like to tell you this morning. You're going to travel abroad and you'll meet a tall dark man who'll –"

"Probably try to sell me insurance."

"All right. Have it your unromantic way. But –" she suddenly sighed though her face held its wrinkled smile, "– what wouldn't I give to be your age and with what has just dropped into your lap. Fairy godmothers was the old-fashioned way. Now its Jones, Jenkins and Appleshaw, Solicitors. But never mind all that." She came forward and kissed Lily on the cheek. Then as she drew back she said, "I

8

don't want any discussion about it. How will I manage and so on. I'll tell you how I will. Two or three weeks just on my own will suit me down to the ground. I'll repaper and repaint the spare bedroom and your room and –" she raised a silencing hand "– don't say a word. I'll get Mr Cape in to help with the heavy side. He's a good worker and I like him."

Lily said, "You're running ahead a bit. I don't know that I'm going to accept this –"

"Idiot!" Aunt Rachel's voice was sharp to near anger. "You'll do it. You can't say no to this. How'd you know the good Lord and some hard-working saint up there haven't gone to a lot of trouble to arrange all this? A real miracle! And you say no. What do you think the good Lord would have said when he parted the waters of the Red Sea for the Israelites to cross over if Moses had said, 'No thanks. We can't walk over them nasty slippery seaweedy rocks and risk broken limbs. We'll try the long way round.' Now – you get in and start on the supper while I finish off this bed. And no nonsense from you." The mock anger went from her suddenly and she reached out a garden gloved hand and took Lily by the elbow and shook her gently, and added. "And don't tell me you're not excited about it. Po-faced you may look, but inside you've got a merry-go round turning away and you riding side-saddle on a white horse waiting for Prince Charming to come along on a black stallion to win and wed and carry you off to his castle. You don't fool me, Lily. You're a good girl – that I know – but you haven't anywhere near given up hope that Mr Right will be along one day and –"

Lily laughed and said, "I'll go and get changed. If he does come riding up tell him I've turned into a frog and you don't know where I've hopped off to."

She leaned forward and kissed her aunt's wrinkled, sunbrowned forehead and then said, "And don't think you can rush me. I haven't said yes to all this yet."

"Oh, yes, you have. But you haven't told me everything, have you?"

9

"How do you mean?"

"You know what I mean. What Mr Porter told me on the telephone when he made the appointment – though he said strictly speaking he shouldn't but he mentioned it in case you made a fuss about coming to see him. Getting all upset that is."

"I never get upset."

"Not that it shows, no. But it sends out waves."

"So what is it?"

"That you could take another girl with you for company."

"Oh, Lord, yes. I forgot that."

"Well, you'd better begin to think about it. You can't go just on your own. That wouldn't be proper. Besides you've got to have someone to talk to and to have a giggle with."

"But I don't know anyone who would come with me. You know I don't have any close friends."

"No, because you spend too much time with me – not that I'm ungrateful but I've tried to make you go out more. You got to have someone to go with. What do you imagine people will think of a good-looking girl like you travelling alone in a first class double cabin?"

"First class?"

Aunt Rachel banged the palms of her hands on her rib sides and said, "Oh, Lily. A double cabin, first class and you alone in it – you think every man on board is going to be an angel, pure in thought, word and deed? You mean to tell me that old Jim Shawcross the baker's man has never pinched –"

"He did it once. You were out shopping. I sent him and his loaves, white and brown, flying. You know I got no time for men anyway."

"The time will come. Give it time and time will bring changes. Your Uncle Albert was always saying that. He said it was the foundation of every true optimist and most men are optimists where good-looking girls like you are concerned. Learn some sense . . ."

Aunt Rachel walked stiffly to the house and, since the

ground was a little damp from recent showers, some mud clung to her gardening shoes. They walked around to the back door so that she could use the garden scraper and brush to clean them off before going into the kitchen.

Lily went upstairs to her room, a low-ceilinged long room with a window at either end, one looking back over the sprawl of houses to Cheltenham and the other facing the rising wooded ground which rose towards the great plateau and the long, straight Roman road that ran south towards Cirencester and the other once great Roman towns – Bath and Silchester. She'd never been any great scholar but she loved reading about history and from reading moving on to a lazy kind of daydreaming in which now and then she felt herself suddenly truly lifted out of the present into the past . . . just a flickering, sometimes mildly eerie and scaring sense of being translated into those old times.

She sat for a moment or two in the window seat before changing into her house shoes and out of her best blouse and skirt into her work-a-day clothes; and, staring at the far distant hilltop trees, had a sudden pang of apprehension . . . like the physical upset of going to a new school, a new job, a new anything which had to be faced and which even though from common sense she knew there was nothing to worry about that she would worry . . . couldn't help it. It was part of her nature. All trains and buses were there to be missed because she was late. She never was. All strangers were there to intimidate her – though they never did after the first few minutes of introduction. Sometimes this way of facing the future annoyed her and she gave herself a good talking to – but it did little good. Faced with anything new . . . then she had rats in her tummy until the actual moment of meeting and then, always to her surprise – though she could never take prior reassurance of its happening – she lost all nervousness and timidity and was suddenly her real self . . . a young woman of common sense, of good presence and, if no great beauty, then at least pleasantly endowed physically and with a good brain and with a fund of kindness and willingness to help others.

Looking at herself in her dressing-table mirror she said aloud suddenly, surprising herself as though the words had come from a complete stranger standing, unknown until then, behind her . . . words which at that moment made little sense to her . . . '*Don't say no to sudden change. No river ever ran that didn't at times burst its banks and take a new course. Life is a river – go with it, not against it.*' Looking at herself in the mirror, she suddenly shook her head and smiled and then said aloud. "What a funny old day. Me going on a cruise. Me with a little money to put in the bank . . ."

As she spoke she looked from her window, out over the back garden with its patch of lawn and then the tidy strip of vegetable garden – lettuce, carrots and three rows of her aunt's beloved perpetual spinach and a row of raspberry canes whose fruit they shared with the birds. Beyond the low boundary a young man came along the path that backed the row of houses. He was bare headed, his fair hair long, and he sported a small neat beard. He wore a brown kaftan sort of cloak or robe and carried a long, rough-cut hazel or ash stave. He glanced aside as he passed the end of the garden and, seeing her standing in the window of her bedroom, buttoning the front of the clean blouse she had put on, he lifted a hand of greeting, touched the closed fingers of his left hand to his lips and blew her a kiss.

To her surprise, as he disappeared, where normally she would have found herself indignant, offended even, prudishly disturbed, she suddenly tipped her head back, caught a glimpse of rooks circling high over the wood-banked distant rise and said to herself, 'Cheeky devil . . .' Then she laughed and, without reason she could name, found herself suddenly happy, carefree, and knowing the rising excitement – not of apprehension as she would have expected about her windfall and going cruising but of suddenly being uplifted and excited at the prospect . . . without trepidation or initial nervousness. The gods had been good to her. All they asked in return was her happiness and a nice little gesture of thanks to Mrs Ellington. Tomorrow she would go to her grave and put flowers there . . . not garden flowers. Though Mrs Ellington liked those well enough, her true love was for wild flowers . . . the flowers of God's own garden, she used to say. Well, tomorrow she would take her small car and drive into the country and see if she could find some flowering furze or gorse . . . either of which stood for enduring affection . . . to put on her grave . . .

At this moment a new and unexpected feeling overcame her. Her head suddenly began to swim a little, muddling her thoughts, and she felt a slow unsteadiness take over her body so that she sat down on the end of the bed and, elbows on knees, held her head between her hands and with a deliberate effort of will fought back against whatever it was that seemed suddenly to have wanted to possess her. As the spell passed and she looked up, raising her head from being cupped in her hands, she saw coming back along the lane the young man who had recently passed down and she knew why he was returning. The lane led nowhere, finished shortly in a dead end. As he passed the end of the garden, he passed without looking in her direction, his head making a little half-nodding motion as though he might have been talking to himself. Stranger, she thought. Had to be. Everyone around here knew that the path came to a dead end.

From the foot of the stairs her aunt's voice came up to her. "I'm going off to Doris's place. We've got all that jumble sale stuff to sort out and price. I'll have a bite of supper with her. I've left the pie in the oven. All you've got to do is to warm it up and do the veg. I got some frozen calabrese – and then there's half the treacle tart left. All right?"

"Yes. Don't worry about me."

"And don't take no for an answer from Suzie."

Lily went out to the head of the stairs and looked down. "What about Suzie?"

13

"Well – who else could you take with you?"

"I don't know. I hadn't given it thought. But she's a bit flighty, isn't she?"

"She's a bit lively, yes. But there's nothing wrong with that. A good laugh and a giggle . . . Oh, and a bit flirty. But full of life. Just what you need . . . you old sobersides. You're twenty-eight – not forty-eight. Mr Right's somewhere round the corner. Perhaps not the first one but one of them not so far off. And that's what Mrs Ellington was thinking about. She liked you. And she knew you. You're grown up but you still don't know what you are. And a lot of people never do discover. Well – then it's a good thing to get out of a rut and do something different for a while . . . something you never dreamed of before." Her aunt laughed and, deliberately teasing, went on, "Can't you see yourself . . . leaning over the ship's rail . . . moonlight on the water . . . a young man at your side, his hand holding yours and you suddenly know what he's going to say, and that he's the one . . . the happy-ever-after man. Golly – I wish it were me."

With a sly look at her aunt, Lily said, "There's always Mr Hector Hopway . . ."

"Hector Hopway? More like Hopaway. You think I'd marry again – and to a man who collects regimental buttons of past and present British regiments? And would expect me to brasso and polish them? And spends hours in his glasshouse talking to his Peppermint Sims and Ballerina and Brocade carnations . . . though I must say they're very lovely and he really has got green fingers."

Lily laughed. "You don't fool me. The moment you got me settled you'd change your tune. So don't worry. It may seem like it but I'm not wanting to finish up an old maid. Mr Right will be along one day."

"How do you know he hasn't been along? Taken a stroll past the house, seen you and said – Oh, dear – she's not a bit like it said in the advertisement."

"Thanks."

Her aunt went to her, put her arms around her gently and,

kissing her cheek, said – "You must allow an old lady a tease. But I'd like to see you married . . . and with children. That's what's for you. Not tapping at a typewriter like I used to do and in a daft way wondering *if* there were a word like *Qwertyuiop* what on earth would it mean? Now I'm off – no, no, I'm not. I just thought of something. Don't take no from Suzie. She and you are a match. If you want to know in what way – well, work it out for yourself. But what you've got, she hasn't, and vice versa, and you've got on well for years . . . quarrelled together, done things together and stuck together, though you're as different as chalk and cheese. So you just ask her."

"When?"

"This evening, of course. Didn't I say? I phoned her this morning and said you'd be on your own for some time this evening and there was enough steak and kidney pie for two and half a treacle tart with cream left. So there you are. Have a nice meal and then tell her the good news and don't take no for an answer – a Mediterranean cruise. All expenses paid. Moonlight and romance and –"

"Seasickness if it's rough."

Her aunt rose. "I give you up. You're too sensible and practical for words. What you want is a large dosage of the unexpected. Well, you've got your first. You're off on a cruise with enough money to enjoy yourself. Right?"

"Right."

"Then take it from there. Nothing in this world happens without a reason. Though it may take some of us years and years to realize what. Now I must rush."

* * * *

Suzie Wilson pushed her chair back from the dining-room table and, raising a warning hand, said cheerfully, "No, you don't. I'll do all the clearing up and put the stuff in the dishwasher. You got the meal – that's fair enough."

"But I don't want you to do anything. You're at it all day

15

long at the shop and then scurrying home to get a meal for your father and brothers."

"True, Lily – but this is different. They just take it all for granted." She laughed, shaking her head so that the evening sunlight through the window took its ashy blondness and gilded it in soft-moving planes of gold leaf.

Such lovely hair, Lily thought – and many times before had thought, though never with any true envy. Suzie was a handsome girl: well built, high complexioned, the fairest of fair hair. There was, Lily always thought, something very Swiss-looking about her. When you saw her coming down the street you thought of farm girls coming across flower-spread Alpine meadows carrying milk pails on those wooden things that went across their shoulders and the cow bells going *ding-ding-ding* in slow time. Maybe she was edging a little to the plump side lately . . . but then a lot of men liked that and, anyway, Suzie liked a lot of men about but there was never any worry about her losing her head over one in the wrong way. She liked men and she liked company, and she could be warm and affectionate perhaps to too many of the wrong type, but she never lost sight of her self-respect and the principles which came naturally to her. A heart of gold and a hand-out to anyone in real want – but let a man take a liberty and he would get first the back of her hand and then the sharp edge of her tongue with now and again the odd, unexpected word mixed in it that would surprise him.

"We'll do it together then," said Lily. "And while we do I'll let you into a surprise. It only come to me this afternoon – when I had to go to the solicitors. You know – about poor Mrs Ellington?"

"There was nothing poor about her. But, bless her soul, she was a good lady."

"Yes, she was. And that's what I want to tell you about. But first let's put this lot in the dishwasher and then I can tell you."

"Is it something good?"

"Yes, it is. Very good."

16

"Then don't keep me waiting. I'm the impatient sort. Tell me now and we'll pack the washer afterwards. Dirty plates never offended me. Four men in the kitchen with a healthy hatred of hot water and dish cloths . . . you should know it. So what is all this?"

"Well. . . ."

Lily drew a deep breath and, leaning forward over the remains of the tart and beaming at Suzie, began to tell her about the visit to the solicitor and the details of the legacy which had been left to her, finishing up, "So you see, everything's paid for and I think a nice thought, too, of Mrs Ellington to not want a girl to go alone on –"

"Aye, that's true. Depending on the girl, of course. Into which category comes neither of us – thank God. Not that I won't marry one day but it'll be a long and spare-nothing lot of thinking before I say 'Yes'. The last thing I would want is anyone like my father or me brothers. Charm the birds off the trees and then pluck and bake 'em for an evening pie, they would. And there's Mrs Wilson round the corner . . . seven kids and a house full of other people's washing and her husband left her these six years and not a word from him. Poor woman. But you wouldn't think so. Always got a laugh and singing away over other people's dirty linen. And the kids! Not a one that isn't full of the devil and they look like angels. And –" Suzie suddenly paused, stared wide-eyed at Lily and said in almost a whisper, "Lily, my love. You mean it, don't you? I mean . . . everything paid for and three weeks away and living like a lady? And all those foreign places?"

Lily said, "You know I mean it. I absolutely mean it."

Suzie put both hands flat across her face masking all but her eyes and shaking her head slowly said, "Wait till I tell them. Not that they're bad as men go, but they never think to raise a hand in the house. Just wait till I tell them – and they'd have to rope me down to keep me there. All the way to the Mediterranean and Italy and Greece and Jerusalem . . . and back . . . and not a plate to wash or cottage pie to make

17

or –" She broke off abruptly and a doleful look flooded her face.

Lily asked, "Are you all right? Was there something wrong with the p –"

Suzie almost wailed, "I've got nothing to wear. Not a thing. They're all dressed up, you know. I've seen the pictures in the travel shop windows."

Lily said sharply, "Stop it, Suzie. All that will be fixed. Whatever you want you can have. She left the tickets and spending money – more than you or I will need."

"She did?" Suzie breathed deeply and wiped away her tears with a tissue. "Ah, she was an angel. Don't you know, angels only come or make things different for people when they're in want or at the end of their tether and they've put up the right kind of prayer. Hail Mary full of Grace . . ." She crossed herself.

Knowing her friend's emotional and sometimes almost immature nature, though this in some ways had always strengthened their friendship, Lily said briskly, "Come on – help me clear away. Then we'll have some coffee and a glass of liqueur and talk sensibly about all this. Stop snivelling. We're going on an all-expense-paid holiday."

Suzie gave a last sniff and then smiled and with a complete change of manner said, "Aye, we'll do that. Holy Mother, what a thing to look forward to. All expenses paid. Spain, Italy, Greece and the Holy Land . . . Jerusalem. Well, let my father and brothers try and talk me out of it. They'll get the edge of my tongue." She paused for a moment or two, a far away look in her eyes as though she were contemplating some fast-forming problem in her mind. Suddenly she wailed, "But I can't go! Who'll clean up and pay the tradespeople?"

Lily gave a small sigh, and said, "Suzie . . . just stop looking for snags. There's nothing that can't be fixed. You're coming with me and we're going to enjoy ourselves. Your menfolk can look after themselves – and maybe that'll teach them what it's like to run a house and cook and clean for a family. Happen you might find that they'll cope much easier than you think. When they know they're on their own they manage . . . it's only when the womenfolk are around that they pretend they don't know how to boil an egg or make a custard. So it's settled then?"

"Yes. Oh, yes, really, Lily. And thanks for thinking of me."

"You were the first one to come into my mind . . . and why not? We've been friends ever since we went to infant school together. Now let's clear all this stuff away and I'll show you the brochure of the cruise . . . and there's a map of all the places we go to."

Later, as Suzie walked home through the deepening gloaming of the late Spring evening, her head was swimming with a fast-moving series of mental pictures of the cruise to come . . . of herself and Lily lying on a sun deck, their bodies gently tanning . . . the call of swooping gulls overhead and on the skyline the growing shape of a headland or mountain overlooking a bay which marked their next port of call . . . maybe one of the ship's officers stopping to talk . . . a tall dark handsome man, sunbrowned, fair-haired and blue-eyed . . . and overhead the gulls crying and a steward coming to them carrying a tray of iced drinks and she not able to decide in her mind which of the two she fancied most . . . mind you, merely now as a pleasing mental exercise . . . the steward with the drinks or the ship's officer. She walked the well known streets to her home, scarcely aware of them, her mind slowly filling with more and more delightful and pleasing images of cruising the Mediterranean. And in this state she turned into the side street of the main road where she lived. But as she did so a leather-geared, white-crash-helmeted motorcyclist came fast and noisily around the corner and headed straight for her.

She gave a high cry of alarm and then felt her right arm taken firmly from behind and herself pulled backwards sharply out of the path of the noisy speeding machine which passed her with its horn blaring away. She almost fell over

19

from the impetus of being drawn back, but a hand held her firmly. She turned round, breathing heavily with shock to find herself looking into the gently smiling, good-natured-looking face of a man wearing a loose blue overall and blue denim trousers. With her heart still pounding from her fright she nevertheless felt the fear going from her as he said, "We were daydreaming, weren't we?"

"I . . . I. . . . I don't know. But thanks ever so much. They're young devils with their bikes some of them. But it was a bit my fault. I was far away."

"A nice daydream?"

He crossed the road with her holding her arm until they reached the far pavement.

She nodded – and later thought how odd it was that her fright seemed to have vanished, no aftermath of shock setting her a-tremble as it might normally have done. Without considering why, just letting the words come spontaneously, almost as though someone else spoke for her, as though they had met before though she knew full well they never had, she repeated: "In a way it was partly my fault. I was day-dreaming . . . I've just had some good news."

"Ah, good news. How nice for you! But that is the time when one should be watchful. Happiness makes us some-times over-trusting." He grinned and there was a twinkle, roguish, almost she thought in his dark hazel eyes. "And when we are like that Old Nick takes a chance with his tricks now and then."

"Well . . . that may be. But accidents is accidents and if they're going to be then they will be, won't they?"

He dropped his arm from her elbow as they stepped on to the far pavement and turned down the road. He said, shaking his head, "No. Nothing is fore-ordained. Life is like a lump of Plasticine. You get it, gifted to you at birth, and from it *you* shape your life. Life doesn't make you."

She grinned suddenly, gave a little laugh and said, "Why didn't someone tell me that before?"

He laughed gently, and then said, "Well, you know now."

20

She commented, unabashed about her curiosity and somehow sensing it would not be resented, "You look kind of Frenchy with that blue blousey thing and blue trousers."

"Well, that's reasonable. I bought them recently on a trip to France."

"Oh – do a lot of travelling do you?"

"A fair amount."

"On business?"

"Mostly."

"I'm going travelling soon. Well . . . cruising with a friend of mine. All over the Mediterranean. You ever been on a cruise?"

"Oh, yes. Often."

"What's it like?"

"Whatever you want to make it. That's the joy – or the temptation. It depends on your nature. A ship is a whole world in miniature – but with one difference."

"What's that."

"It's a nicer world than this one. People aren't so horrid to one another. Everyone's friendly and kind. Oh, a few are rather stuck-up and show-offs but in a way that does no harm. You'll be all right, I'm sure."

"I'm glad to hear that. You know when you've never done something before you get sort of rats in your tummy."

"Of course you do. But that's part of it all. A little anxiety beforehand is only the sprinkle of salt needed to make a well-cooked meal perfect." He paused, his hand just re-straining her by the arm, and said, "Well, here you are. Home – safe and sound. And it's been very nice talking to you."

"And me to you. And thanks about the motor-bike."

"Nothing. But you watch out in future. Save your daydreaming from off the streets." He gave her a smile, put out a hand and just touched her left shoulder and then was away down the street without once looking back. As he turned the far corner she gave a little sigh and went into the house.

Her father looked up from his evening paper and said, "Who was that bloke?"

"What bloke?"

"I had to go to the window where I'd left my pipe and baccy –" he held up his hands, pipe in one the tobacco tin in the other – "for my evenin' smoke and I see'd you with him. Looked a kind of well . . . holy Joe sort. He trying to touch you for cash . . . some charity? Could have been a faker, you know. They're about. Charity. But for who? Themselves, of course. What did he touch you for?"

Without knowing why Suzie said, "Five pounds."

"What? He never did!"

"Twas for a good cause. They want to start a home for three-legged ostriches."

Her father squinted at her over the end of his pipe and then with a slow grin said, "Oh, like that, is it? Mind your own business – but wait for the surprise. Well – so long as it isn't to tell me that you're going to get married and leave home . . . me and the two lads stranded and neither of them able to do more than hard fry an egg and burn a rasher of bacon."

"That's right. I'm leaving home – but only for about three weeks. So why don't you and the boys go and book in at the Royal Albert Hotel. You all spend enough time in the bar down there you might as well only have to take a lift up to your bedrooms rather than tipsy-wipsy walk through the dangerous streets home of a night."

Her father, wide-eyed with surprise, looked at her silently for a while and then, with an unexpected smile, said, "Well, well – it's happened at last. The worm's turned. Bully for you lass. It'll do the lads good." He shook out his paper, turned a page and lowering his eyes to read, added, "I knew you 'ad it there somewhere – a touch of your mother's sharp spirit. And no bad thing. So, when you want to tell me all about it I'll be waitin' and, whatever it is, you'll get my blessin'."

Suddenly grinning to herself Suzie went to him, leaned over and kissed him on the forehead.

TWO

JOHN EGGERTON CAREFULLY turned over the two
eggs frying in the pan to close their eyes, counted ten and
took them out so that the yokes should not be cooked hard,
and put them on his supper plate in the electric heater
underneath the window. He looked out over the sprawl of
houses. Straight ahead he could see a well kept garden of
lawns and flower beds and beyond a high brick boundary
wall over which he could just see the county cricket ground
where he spent much time when on leave in the summer. To
the right he could see the trim building of the Royal
Southampton Yacht Club of which he was a very privileged
member. It was convenient for him to pop over and join his
fellow members for his pre-lunch drink. Sometimes he
stayed for lunch with a guest or a party of his friends at their
invitation.

It was a view his wife had enjoyed before her death five
years ago. She always felt she could see where he was when
on leave, and this would make up for the times when she was
too unwell to accompany him.

John Eggerton was every inch a seaman, like his father
and indeed his grandfather. His father had been a ship's
engineer as his father before him; John's grandfather had
gone down in the *Titanic*. He could remember being taken by
his father to the marine museum on the quayside to see the
memorabilia of the *Titanic* and he sometimes, even now,
revisited the place, feeling a glow of pride in his family
connection with the great liners and the sea and Southampton Water.

23

It was not surprising that as soon as he had left the grammar school he had wanted to go to sea and his father apprenticed him to one of the cruisers as a ship's engineer.

Father lived only a few years after his retirement, 'Being a landlubber' did not suit him and his mother always said that 'Father died of a longing for the sea'. John Eggerton – who had a touch of poesy and whimsy about his thinking and reveries – mused 'he went out on the tide at sunset . . . floating down the rays of the setting sun, seabound and for sure destined to be heaven-harboured at the end of that last journey.'

Things changed too quickly these days. It was five years since his wife had died; five years he had lived alone heartbroken. Certainly no other woman had ever raised one moment of desire or envy in him. None of his activities, community or charitable, had ever filled the gap she left. He grinned, deprecating his self pity, dropped two rashers of bacon into the pan and let his eye run over the rooftops, southwards towards the docks. Away towards Southampton he could clearly hear the great dredgers working away clearing the silt and mud from the docks, the deep grunting and groaning – like a giant with the bellyache, he mused. In a few days he would be out there again, on the sea, on another voyage, a hardened and ardent cruiser – and why not? Shorebound people were too tied up with their immediate business and family affairs. But on shipboard they opened like the sudden sun and flower burst of an alpine meadow, flowerheads thrusting through even the snows of the higher slopes . . . red, blue, purple and yellow . . . all cocking a snook at departing winter and raising their heads to take the long-lacked warmth of spring and nearing summer.

He reached out for the whisky bottle that stood with his empty glass on the window sill. He filled the glass to the top of the reeds – which were engraved decoratively around the glass to about half its height. *Up to the reeds and no more. Three times and that's it.* No over indulgence. No extra little one because it's been a good or a bad day. Every day had to be one or the other. Okay. Up to the reeds. Twice had been enough when Clarice was alive. Perhaps three for a birthday or some special occasion. Well . . . well . . . Each man kills the thing he loves . . . some do it with a word and some do it with a sword. True. And some do it with a glass and the still not shaken off slow resentment that life had given brief happiness and then snatched it back.

"Ah-la-la . . ." he suddenly said aloud, reaching for his glass. "Here we go again. Money in the bank, a nice flat, a secure job doing what you like – but you miss a woman. Not any woman, but *the* woman. Not just sex. But the other thing . . . knowing she's there. Knowing you stand as big in her thoughts as she stands in yours. And . . . Oh, leave it you'll have yourself blubbering in a few moments."

He took a sip of his whisky then dished up his eggs and bacon and put the meal in the warming drawer . . . the ritual fixed for years and welcome. Second whisky at hand, hot meal into the warming drawer. Whisky finished. Fix third. Sit in window armchair and drink it watching the promenade of folks you knew in the city . . . this city which had been his, man and boy, for forty years or so. In summer the passers-by were lightly dressed for cricket or tennis at the club or mothers with children visiting Chipperfields Zoo on the common running beside the famous Avenue. In the winter folk wrapped against the rain and heads lowered against the wind. You could sit and watch it all for a while and perhaps get a little bit tiddly and talk to yourself . . . Poor old you.

From his chair in the window embrasure he watched the few bad-weather harassed passers-by make their way along the road . . . head and shoulders bent low against the rain-filled wind blowing gustily, shaking the tall trees and the rhododendron and magnolia bushes which grew in abundance in the usually kind Southampton climate.

He took a sip of whisky and hugged his shoulders slightly together in a movement of pleasure and self congratulation.

25

Here he was, warm and comfortable in his own flat, while outside were people walking heads down against the rain and wind, going perhaps back to homes and lodgings where neither comfort nor companionship waited . . . or where no matter the luxury of being comfortably off there was a poverty of human congress . . . no true friends, no real loved one . . . so many people bereft of the commonplace human furnishings of everyday normal life.

And just then, as though the train of his thinking had in some miraculous way made her materialise, he saw his married sister come along the road below mackintoshed, umbrella held low against the wind. She halted opposite the block of flats and looked up. Knowing she could see him, he raised a hand in greeting and turned back from the window. His sister Margery . . . fair-haired, blue-eyed . . . as pretty as a picture though perhaps a little of the original colouring had faded now at thirty plus, with a husband who was an idle dreamer and in practical matters far from honest given a chance to be so with some gullible soul. But worse still . . . was violent in frustration or want, readier with a bruising hand than a respected show of fortitude in adversity. In short, John Eggerton thought: thoroughly useless and unworthy and the tragedy of his sister's life, and a source of wonder to him that she had ever married such a creature. But . . . there you were. What other people did, be they men or women, so often defeated the imagination.

A few minutes later he went to the front door of the flat, opened it and walked across the common hall that served the other three flats and waited, hearing the whine of the lift and then the clang and jolt of its arrival at his floor.

The doors drew back and she stepped out and, surprisingly for a moment or two, she took him back years to the time when they were both in their twenties. Her hat off, her fair hair wind blown, her cheek flushed and healthy and the smiling lips cherry ripe and free of lipstick. He suddenly saw her at eighteen, flushed from tennis, dropping into a deck chair and reaching out a hand for the glass of lemonade from

26

one of her many suitors. And with all that choice she had to make the wrong one.

A few minutes later she was seated before the wall-mounted electric fire, a large gin and tonic in her hand – sipped at, but taken only to please him and probably never to be finished – her face shining still from the wind and rain, her fair hair and blue eyes, angelic, the prettiness a little faded – not for good – but from lack of happiness. Mrs Richard Chambers – Mr Richard Chambers being a comfortably situated proprietor of a tobacconist and sweet-shop on the approach to the city – his sister was known always to him as Marg, very near his own age but far less capable and, acknowledged even by herself, one of the world's worst choosers. Eight times out of ten she picked badly or unwisely . . . whether it concerned vegetables or groceries or fashions or friendships and – without a doubt – love and marriage. So bad was her luck or her selection of people or things – she would buy curtain material and work for a week to put them up in the sitting-room or a bedroom and then find that they made the most awful contrast with the carpet or wallpaper. If she gave a small supper or dinner party something would go wrong. Going wrong was the demon that haunted her life. He, himself, could have a little touch of sympathy for her husband, but not to the point of even remotely condoning the man's brutality.

He refilled his own glass and sat down opposite her. They both drank . . . a token sip . . . a fleeting ritual and then she said flatly, "I've left him – for good."

"For good?" It was an idiotic response but for the first time between them he needed thinking space.

"For good. Can you put me up?"

"Of course. What happened?"

"You'll never believe it."

"You know I will. But whatever it is I just hope to God you mean it – that you're never going back. . . . There's always this place."

She laughed, briefly and rejectingly. "I came back

unexpected. I got the dates of a W.I. meeting mixed. Went and found the place shut up. So I came back and there he was in our bed with another woman. As bold as brass – and the woman hardly less so. In fact I'm surprised they didn't ask me to make coffee for them. . . . Oh, John! I've had it! Just had it! All right, he doesn't love me – but why humiliate me . . . treat me like dirt?"

He said quietly, reaching out and taking her hand, "Forget all that. We'll get it all fixed up. A divorce – and I'll see that he makes proper allowance for you."

"Bless you . . . Oh, God, I feel so awful running back to you. But this last thing has been all too much. I feel I just want to go right away . . . from everything and forget that I ever had a life with him. Two months' happiness I had and then his true colours came through. He's a sadist, John. A sadist. I'm not exaggerating. I think he'd like to take me and torture me slowly to death. And for no reason. I've never given him cause. It's as though he has to do it. A disease . . . a kink in his mind."

He got up and refilled his glass and, his back to her, said, "Just calm down and relax. I'm taking over. Tomorrow you can give me a list of what you want and I'll go up and get it. You've got a key still?"

"Yes."

"Then I'll do it while he's at his office. I wouldn't trust myself with him yet. Maybe, perhaps you ought to come too and get all you want."

"But you don't want me here all the time, John."

"I certainly do. For as long as you want to stay."

"Well, I'll be able to look after things while you're away. We can work it all out after that."

"No. You don't stay here while I'm away on the next cruise. I'll phone the agents tomorrow to see if I can book a cabin for you. You're going right away from that sod, from here, and you're going to forget it all. After the cruise . . . well, we'll have no trouble in making some arrangement that suits us both."

"But you don't want me on –"
"I want you. Say no more."

*   *   *   *

In the angle between the blank end of the bar and the outside wall of the bar-room was a small triangularly shaped wooden table that fitted into the corner of the bar-room with just enough room for two people to sit around two of its equilateral sides. Its third side was hard against the bar-room wall radiator and a great cascading growth of maiden hair fern which tumbled from a pot on a small wall bracket . . . Maisie's pride and joy it was – Maisie being the wife of Joe Grey, the proprietor of the Honeypot Inn. Childless Maisie had developed a passion for pot plants that near turned the saloon bar into a tropical conservatory . . . God help anyone who thought to be funny and water any of them with a glass of whisky or gin . . . though a little real ale administered *by herself* was a different thing. Maisie loved her family of plants.

Childless, not even married, also was ex-Captain Frank Langton living in a small flat on his pension and a little capital, enough – as he frequently remarked in public – to keep him from starving but not enough to enable an old soldier who had given his life to serving Queen and Country to afford a wardrobe fit for a gentleman or to drink a glass of wine of a decent vintage every night with his dinner . . . who wanted wine that came from a plastic holder through a plastic tap and spouted into a bastard imitation plastic wine glass? All right, he might not ever have been commissioned into the officer ranks, but in the mess in his day – though nothing could take the place of beer – they drank wine as well. That they did. All the way up from Salerno, through Rome, Cassino and to the foot of the Alps. And no matter how rough the going, there was never any excuse for a sloppy turnout once you got back from the front line. Take pride in yourself and stick to the truth – against these there can be no denial. He was a mine of old saws and proverbs and other pieces of homespun wisdom. Though where he got them no one knew, for he was not a great reading man . . . he was a ready spinner of tales, some true, most apocryphal – and the apocryphal ones usually featured himself in the role of hero or wise counsellor.

He was, as Maisie often said to his face, 'A lovely man – and who cares a bugger if he's the biggest liar in the world? Give me lies, lovely, gorgeous lies. I've had enough reality'. She would declaim this at full voice from behind the bar unfailingly at least once during the evening and usually just before closing time.

But there was much more to Captain Frank Langton than a large talking braggart living forever in a past which every year he embellished with more and more exploits and chivalrous deeds which were far from the truth . . . which were the wishful creation of an active desire to make of his humdrum, far from valorous past, a saga of hard campaigns, dashing exploits and a disregard for his own skin in the saving of others in danger. Everyone who knew him in the bar knew the truth about him but liked and tolerated him because fundamentally he was a likeable man and addition-ally he could tell a good, if fictional, anecdote about his own career with verve and gusto – and, above all this, he was possessed of an innate kindness, so impulsive that he was a soft touch for anyone with a hard-luck story. As Maisie was fond of saying in his absence, "He needs someone to look after him – some good woman. There's them that comes in here have touched him for a loan and never even thought of paying it back. Oh, I know it may only be a few bob or so . . . but put enough fews together and you end up with a sizeable sum. He's got a a good heart – and I'll say this for him – he can tell a good story about his doings and seeings and what matter if there's little enough truth to them?"

This evening instead of sitting at his table and chatting with the changing bar company while he had three halves of his favourite bitter, he sat for one drink and then rose to go, giving Maisie a smile and a *good night*.

Maisie said, "You're off early tonight, Captain."

"Going to meet Mrs Bell at the station. Been up to London she has."

"A shopping spree, eh?"

"Dunno. She don't tell me anything until it's happened like. Thought I'd walk her back from the station. She'll have done some shopping and need help."

After he had gone out a man at the end of the bar – young, brash, a car salesman of the too slick, too smart, and not-too-honest type said with a wink, "Can't think why them two don't get married. Use one flat instead of two, let the other and there you are . . . a bit of good for both of them."

Maisie said, acidly, "Why don't you suggest it to the Captain? He's always ready to listen to good advice – though of course, he might give you a smack on the nose for sticking it into his business."

"Think so? Nah . . . he's a lot of big talk. Nice guy, mind you. But all big talk. '*I was at Monte Cassino . . . I was this and I was that.*' All very interesting but he was probably tucked away safe, miles down the rear. Mind you, he's nice enough, but – well, he isn't or ever will be a hero."

"I don't want to discuss my customers with you. So change the subject."

But Captain Frank Langton would have agreed with him. He was not the stuff of which heroes were made. He wished he were – but he was just the opposite. He was, and had been principally, a peacetime regular soldier with no experience of the real thing until the war came and then, knowing his own lack of true courage, had managed to arrange his career so that he kept out of the front lines in North Africa and Italy and hated every moment of his fear. He was – and he regretted it – not of the stuff which seeing a runaway horse galloping down a street, where schoolchildren were crocodile-crossing a road, would have rushed out and grabbed the horse's halter and fought it to a standstill. Ah, if he were, he used to think. . . . But that was not the way God had made him. Not that he blamed God. He had no time for that kind of self-pity or arrogance. He was the way God had ordained he should be and there was no quarrelling with Him.

The local branch train from the main line station was ten minutes late, which surprised him not at all. They were, seeing the way the railways were these days, lucky still to have a branch connection from the main London line. Ten minutes late was nothing. He waited close to the exit from the platform and knew, as he had long known, because he had waited for Mrs Bell many times before, the slowly growing elation of seeing her again. Again . . . one would have thought that weeks had elapsed when it was only this morning that he had walked her down to the station to go off to London. She owned her own house and had turned it into three flats. The bottom one she lived in. Above that lived the science mistress from the local girls' grammar school, and in the top flat he lived like an attic mouse but with a view over the roofs of the small country town to the chalk downs where once the Danes had marched to meet King Alfred and his warriors . . . and he lived a happy man, full of dreams of what he would have liked to have been . . . sometimes even claiming experiences and feats which were apocryphal . . . but no matter – given the chance he could have, he was sure, made them a reality. Well, some of them . . . ah, well, perhaps not. He was no hero.

He heard the train coming and in the growing dusk moved to stand under one of the station lights so that she should see him. Though she had never said so, he guessed that, when she saw him waiting, her pleasure was the same as his. Lots of other things he guessed, which pleased them both remained hidden one from the other. He wished that he had the courage to speak of some of them but somehow could never bring himself to the point of framing the right words. He guessed, too that she took his army reminiscences for what they were . . . highly coloured . . . with himself the hero

32

he would have liked to have been . . . with himself who, at the height of a crisis with all the other officers killed, took command and held the line with a surviving handful of men until reinforcements arrived. He had been a good, competent peacetime regular soldier but had seen little real warfare and had liked none of it. But now in his sixties he looked back and saw his past war years painted in bright hues and dark shadows . . . all vivid and dramatic and himself in the thick of every action.

They walked together the short distance from the station to Mrs Bell's house, he carrying her bulging shopping bag and, with his free hand, helping her up the narrow rise of steep steps from the road to the cobbled walk that ran along the front of Chantry Terrace with its red-bricked, narrow four-storied houses overlooking the yew-lined walk of the path that ran from the lych gate beyond the last house up to the great high-steepled parish church, whose clock had for years marked the uneventful and often lonely years of her life . . . since that day when she had turned away from her husband's grave, dropping her posy of his favourite wild flowers into it . . .

Frank Langton now squiring her, kindly and always ready to be of service, was not a man of courage as her husband had been. In fact she had long realized that there was in him a core of cowardice which, hating it himself he tried to banish by converting the banal truths of his unexciting war experiences into colourful and stirring episodes. She wouldn't say that he was a coward out and out, but there was a touch of cowardice in him which, added to his own inner diffidence, made him seem to be either a little mild and retiring or, after a glass or two of drink, a bold, though far from braggart, raconteur of his own invented war and life time experiences. Still, she thought, as they walked through the gloaming and the church steeple clock began to strike nine and as this man at her side would have said for he was a great one for proverbs – *if wishes were horses then beggars would ride*. One day – when he could convince himself that he was

33

worthy of her (about which at this moment she did not care tuppence and wished she could tell him so frankly) – he would find the courage to ask her to marry him and she would say *Yes*. It was not a day which she could promote, but the day would come – she had to have faith in that. And looked at sensibly . . . well, two could live cheaper than one. Her flat was large enough and she could, if they shared it as man and wife, re-let the top flat. Suddenly as they went over the awkwardly cobbled footpath to the front door of her house – and in view of what had happened to her today – she made up her mind to give him a little longer to find the courage and the moment to come to the point and, if he didn't, well . . . she would do it herself and make it seem as though it had come from him. That wouldn't be difficult. But above all things first – she would like it to come genuinely and spontaneously from him . . . a love match, not a partnership against growing old and loneliness. But, of course, like all men he had to be handled right. Things had to seem to come from them. They had this pride . . . nursing the myth that they were in charge . . . the strong ones, the organizers. Dear, dear . . . she would have to handle him very carefully over this new thing which had suddenly come into her life – but she knew the line which would convince him that with pleasure there was a strong streak of duty, of the chivalry a woman could call on from any man of spirit and feeling. Although she really loved him, she knew that, like most men, he wouldn't want things taken out of his hands which – in a way – was something she had done today . . . done because she had no one else she could share her luck with – or want to – and also because surely in the course of time sharing her good fortune the real moment of truth would come. She sighed gently . . . wondering whether she was doing right. Men could be very contrary about things because they had this knack of getting things wrong, of seeing things differently from the way they had been meant.

Fifteen minutes later sitting in her front parlour, he with a whisky and she with a small liqueur glass of Cointreau she said, "Frank, I've got something to tell you – but I want you to promise not to be cross about it if you don't like it."

"Why should I be cross?"

"Well, because I think I've taken a big liberty – on your behalf that is, Frank."

He grinned. "Well, if you have, my dear Nancy, I'm sure it will be from the best of reasons. You know I trust you in every way."

She nodded faintly, thinking how after all these years he was still so diffident. Only rarely did he call her by her first name, Nancy. More often he avoided it with a 'my dear' even on high days and holidays when they might have shared a half bottle of wine over dinner at the local hotel – The White Swan – and they walked homewards and he held her arm in the gloaming. But always just fractionally short of the point when she longed for him to kick down the barrier of his pride, his unreasonable (she guessed) assessment of his own worthiness . . . perhaps even of his thinking more than anything else of the warming economical practicality of two being able to live cheaper together than separately. Which was true, of course, and she would have found nothing off-putting in such frankness because – though she felt he was far from sure about it – she loved him and she knew that he loved her. But she sensed that he would never get to the point of open declaration until he had cleared something inside him . . . some shame, some secret self-condemnation, something, she felt, that was small enough as far as the world was concerned but loomed large with him.

She said, "You know how I do these competitions in that women's magazine I take?"

He grinned. "I should do. Ten years I've been here and never a week you've missed and not a sausage have you won. You're like me, my dear, not born for the easy prizes in life. I been doin' the football pools for years. I won once – a big pay-out. Two pounds and fifty pence. But I still keep at it."

"This wasn't like that. This was a fashion competition. There were ten famous film and stage stars . . . women of

35

course . . . and ten pictures of evening gowns by various famous fashion designers and you had to say which dress was for which star."

"Those things are always rigged, love."

"You think so?"

"Certain. You'd do better to take up the football pools and put your crosses where you fancy."

"Well, I don't think so. And I've got news for you –" She gave him a warm smile.

Watching her, there was a sudden pang in him because behind that smile he could suddenly see like the swift movement of a film the various Nancy Bells there had been . . . from a blonde schoolgirl . . . young bride . . . and late in life a good-looking and desirable widow with her looks still holding and maturing into the fine features of a woman of character and charm. And he loved her, but though she might, probably did, guess it, he would never proclaim it because he knew that he was not worthy of her. Oh . . . their relationship now was all right because it had its proper and respected limits. But he was not for her. He bragged a little of army exploits that were fiction, he bullied a little anyone who was overawed by his commanding figure and presence, and he definitely felt himself a cut above many of his town acquaintances. He had served but had never truly suffered for King and Country. At heart he knew himself. He was a coward and – given the chance – more than a bit of a bully. He was never over-unkind but he did enjoy the power of a little authority.

He said: "What kind of news? Good, I hope?"

"Very good. I won a magazine competition. But I'll never understand why I did. I just put the numbers of all the gowns in a basin, muddled them round and then pulled them out one by one – and got them all right."

Frank smiled. "Fortune favours the fair. I'm delighted for you. What was the prize?"

"Well . . . that's where it's a bit difficult."

"Why?"

36

"Well, you know I don't have any close friends in this town. I used to, but over the years they've moved away and a few have died. Oh, I know a lot of people – but not anyone that I would want to go on a Mediterranean cruise with."

"What's a cruise got to do with it?"

"That was the first prize. A first class cruise for the winner and friend . . . all round the Mediterranean . . . and shore excursions . . . Malta, Cyprus . . . Athens, Greece and Israel . . . Haifa, I think it is – I've got the details in my shopping bag. And from there a coach trip to the Dead Sea and Jerusalem." She suddenly looked up and across to him and her face was clouded with worry.

He said, "What you looking sad about, me dear? You'll have the time of your life."

"Well, you see the cruise is for two . . . a deluxe double cabin or two singles . . . all first class . . . and the friend doesn't have to be another woman necessarily. I mean you and I could go. In fact. . . ."

She broke off suddenly and he saw at once the glint of starting tears in her eyes.

He said gently, "What's the matter, my dear?"

"Well . . . I couldn't think of anyone . . . any woman I would want to go with – but then . . . since it didn't have to be a wo –"

He laughed and broke in on her words, saying, "Don't tell me. I can guess. You said – could you bring me?"

"How do you know that?"

"Because if I was in the same fix I'd have said could I bring you and –"

"You're right. But you will come, won't you?"

"Why not? See something again of old places . . . Gibraltar . . . Italy . . . Ay, that was a time. All the way up from Anzio to Monte Casino . . . Florence and Bologna and driving the Hun back to the Alps . . . and few days passing when there wasn't some well-known face missing from the roll call. I tell you . . ."

His words tailed off and she looked at him anxiously and

37

then said quietly, "Is there something wrong, Frank?"

He shook his head and said slowly, "No, not really. Only sometimes thinking back I seem to see it all different from what it was. To be truthful . . . well, sometimes I get twisted up between what was truth and what I've imagined it all was since then. Like sometimes –" He grinned suddenly (and she was touched by the small smile and contrite pursing of his lips . . . a little boy about to confess to a fib) "you could swear it was all like that . . . short commons and hard fighting. Maybe, I suppose, because now with it all long past you have to make it seem romantic . . . forget the real dirt and hardship and every now and then some well-known face missing for ever."

She said, "I can imagine. But – let's forget that. You will come, won't you?"

He was silent for a moment or two and then, the small smile on his face suddenly boyish and almost mischievous, he stood up, came to attention with a click of his heels, gave a little bow of his head and said, importantly, "Madam, I shall be honoured . . . honoured and delighted . . . unworthy though I am of such kindness."

And as he stood there, looking down at her, the warmth of her kindness almost a material, cloaking comfort around him, he would have given anything to push the opportunity further and tell her of his love for her and would she do him the great honour of. . . . Ah, yes. That's what he wanted – but, though her kindness was one thing, the other was much bigger. She could like him, but she also knew him – and knew that behind his talk lay not the hero he would have people think he was but just an ordinary, not very brave, man, who had a healthy respect for his own skin and comfort.

She smiled and, to his surprise stood up suddenly, put her hands on his shoulders and reached up and gave him a little peck of a kiss on his left cheek, wondered for a couple of moments whether he would draw her closer to him, then knew he would not and so stepped back and said, "You're a lovely man . . . Oh, dear, all the way home I was wondering how you would take my forwardness – but who else could I –"

"That's enough. I'm delighted and I'm honoured, ma'am."

Then for a moment or two before he leaned and kissed her good night on the cheek he saw himself reflected in her warm hazel eyes . . . a small, distant figure and thought . . . I could ask her now. Just blurt it out. But friendship is one thing. Marriage now . . . no, that calls for a looking up to . . . each to the other. He loved her – but she knew him too well, knew his inner weaknesses and timidities . . . and they stood in the way and would stay in the way until he had really proved himself to her, to his own, not to her, satisfaction.

She said. "They're going to send all the brochures and stuff about the cruise from the magazine. I can't wait to have them. Think of it. Think of it . . . all those days cruising on the sunny Mediterranean."

His smile broadened. "I know, I know . . . Oh my dear, you were good to think of me." For a moment or two there was a silence between them and he wondered again about asking her, but found the will to do it even weaker. For that moment he knew he would have to have some inner strength, confidence . . . call it what you would . . . that would take him into the declaration of love and devotion without a moment's hesitation because he would know that he had earned the right at least to ask out of worthiness.

Then, on a sudden impulse, undeniable and totally unexpected and alien to him, he said, "Think I'll take a few minutes stroll . . . think things over . . . calm myself down . . . you've been so good . . . breath of fresh air. Don't worry about locking up. I'll do that for you and leave the key in the hall . . ."

He went out into the velvety early summer night and walked along the cobbled path to the dead end of the small sidestreet that ran alongside the wall of the churchyard. He went through the small side gate into the churchyard, its great yews, ebony black against the starlit sky, flanking the path to the church porch, the great spire thrusting into the heavens topped with a tiny red glow of light as a warning against low-flying aircraft.

A reasonably regular if conventional attender at the church, though one who often found his mind wandering during the sermon, he took great pleasure in the singing of hymns since he had a pleasant, though untrained, voice, though he had always drawn a limit to the degree of bawdiness he would countenance, he had always taken more comfort in the act of being present and worshipping than he had in listening to the sermon. More sustaining to him was the act of being alone in church . . . alone with his own thoughts and with the comfort or anguish of his own prayers. Tonight he brought with him the need for thanksgiving and the need for the discovery of true strength to make him worthy of the one prize he wanted from life.

He sat in a high-back pew, the far altar dimly lit, the great brass cross and Christ crucified boldly lit by two slim candelabra flanking it. He leaned forward on his knees, this man of war and little master of his timidity, this gentle person who would like to have been a knight in shining armour and come to the rescue of his beloved – only to find it happening the other way round; this modest-in-mind but sometimes braggart-in-tongue man not greatly endowed with courage and only modestly and incompletely aware of his own potential now did, as so many do, sit and bow his head and find himself bereft of words with which to implore Him to look down and . . . if He had time . . . to sort things out a little . . . perhaps a little more in mitigation of his present situation.

And as he sat there, head bowed, any coherent flow of words or thoughts of supplication far from his command, only the great roll of spiritual upset stirring inside him like a whirlpool of harnessed power turning on the lip of dis-solution into the clear, steady flow of purpose and direction of an on-flowing stream . . . a stream of the days still to come in his life. Though he lacked the words he felt the need and

40

somehow knew that the minor agony of suffering had to be his before anything else.

He sat, head held in his hands until he heard, to his surprise since it was late, the sound of footsteps coming down the centre aisle. As they neared him he raised his head slightly out of curiosity to see a young man in his late twenties or early thirties, dressed slightly hippie style, a long shirt-like tunic falling to his knees, a small beard, hard trimmed, capping his chin, his hair long but – despite the place – the captain in Frank Langton noticed that the man was neat and tidy and, out of respect for another worshipper, he walked by without a look in Frank's direction. This was God's house and anyone in it sat in his own inviolate place.

The man passed him and a little later Captain Langton got up and went out into the night. It was as he walked back to the house that he suddenly realized that it was one thing to go on a paid-for cruise around the Mediterranean – but, even with all meals and accommodation paid for on the cruise ship, there were out-of-pocket expenses as well . . . shore trips came extra, and shopping for souvenirs, and pre-meal drinks and wine at dinner. If you sat around a table of six or eight people and most drank wine . . . well then you had to join in and do likewise . . . particularly as Mrs Bell liked a glass of Chablis or Burgundy with her food. And then there would be other out-of-pocket expenses.

For a moment or two he felt gloomy, then suddenly his mood changed – as though someone somewhere had thrown a switch to boost extra cheer through him. He remembered his brother Will's gold cigarette case. Brother Will . . . two years his senior, married, well-off, though it would have been hard to say what he did to achieve that state so one had to accept his own definition which was, '. . . a little bit of this and a little bit of that and a touch of the other – and always count your change, 'cos the world is full of rogues'. And he had died, as it seemed, without rhyme or reason, dropping dead as he pruned his roses . . . to be precise . . . his favourite rose, *Gloire de Dijon*. Some years ago he had had the case

41

valued and had been told that it was worth seventy-five pounds. Today it ought to be worth twice that price . . . a hundred and fifty pounds? Well, that with a little from what he called his emergency funds and he should be able to get by . . . and the old pension. Not riches, but he could manage. . . . Funny that chap in the church so late. Not a local, he thought. He'd know one of those. Holiday visitor? Could be. Odd, though: the glimpse he'd got of his face gave him the feeling that he'd seen him before somewhere.

He walked back to the house, let himself in, locked up and went up to his flat. An hour later, in bed, on the verge of sleep, he remembered the young man in the church and thought again . . . Funny. Seen that face somewhere before. Never forget a face – though you can't always put a name to 'em. But somewhere . . . yes, somewhere he'd . . . he'd seen . . . Sleep took him and he drifted away – his last cogent thought being . . . sea sickness . . . Oh, Lord he always got that, only for a day and a night . . . but . . . but must get some sea sickness pills . . . seanickness pills . . . peanickness ills . . . sillnickness peas . . .

Close by, the owls that lived in the church tower called to one another and the young man (not all that young . . . maybe thirty odd) walking down to the station to catch the half past midnight train heard them and smiled to himself and remembered the elderly type who had been sitting in the church all by himself. He had a good face . . . one an artist might like to draw . . . a face you could trust, though there was a little touch of weakness somewhere about the mouth. Still . . . he quoted to himself – *There was a passport in his very looks.* . . . Oh, dear – how long ago had it been that he had met the gentleman who had written that? He had known all about sentimental journeys.

Distantly down the valley the train called and a great shooting-star scarred the sky and the young man smiled and said to himself – 'So many things of great beauty and delight in this world . . .'

THREE

THE THREE OF them watched the car drive away . . .
father and two brothers waving from the top of the front
doorsteps and farther along the street the odd housewife and
out-of-work husband, not to mention a few children,
simulating illness to keep them away from school for the day,
and various other bodies, mostly female, leaning out of top
windows or standing in their front gardens, some with small
children at their feet, these waving too but unconcerned at
having no idea why. Mum was doing it so why shouldn't
they?

But the three, father and two sons, now sole occupants of
the Wilson house, waved too but rather more briefly than the
rest of the watchers, and, once the car turned the street
corner, wasted no time in retiring indoors.

Mr Wilson dropped into his armchair, began to fill a pipe,
and said, "Well, that's Suzie off. And if anyone here isn't
truly wishing her a good time don't let me hear of it or they'll
get a slap around the kisser that will be a revelation to them.
Turn and turn about is the order of the day from now on. Jim
you're on upstairs duty . . . bed-making, dusting, slopping
out, brushing down, hoovering and bathroom and lavatory
sanitary work."

"And me?" asked the other son.

"You, Cecil, are on the downstairs shift starting off. You
change over with Jim tomorrow and so on."

"What's the downstairs shift, then?" asked Cecil.

"Very interesting one. You does all the cooking we might
need of an evening. Breakfast – everyone on his own for his

43

own. So you see I don't mean to be idle, 'cos in addition I shall be general supervisor. Mind you, when we feel like it we might have a snack at the pub. But over and above all I want this place kept shipshape and Bristol fashion just like your lucky and very much loved sister 'as left it. Get it?"

Cecil grinned and said, "I could join the Army."

"With flat feet and weak eyes and a weaker 'ead?"

Jim said, "Why don't we go and stay at a hotel? Like the Star and Dog?"

Both his father and his brother laughed and shook their heads. And then his father said, "My boy, you 'ave my full permit to do so. But just one thing bothers me. What will you use for money?"

"Suzie left us a hundred quid house-keepin' and then there's the dole. I could get by."

"You could get the flat of my hand, lad. That's what you could get. That money belongs to us all. So it stays with us all. And that means me. I holds the purse. So – now all that's settled. Just 'cos Suzie gets lucky – bless her 'eart – that don't mean the family breaks up. Whatever would your dead mother 'ave thought?"

"That things was still pretty normal round 'ere."

"Then let's keep 'em like that. But first –" their father suddenly grinned and winked at them, "– let's do the proper thing by our Suzie and wish her bonny voyagin'. There's four bottles of stout in the larder."

The four bottles were duly produced, the crown corks eased off and, without ceremony of glasses, they all drank Suzie's health and happiness on the cruise with a great deal of glugging and wiping of lips with the back of their hands and, since they had wetted their thirst, they decided to go and get rid of it completely before coming back to deal with the household chores.

"Incorrigible," their father said – who had a fondness for the odd long word, though he was not always sure of its meaning. "That's what we are. It's a sign of an artist

44

temperament. Always wantin' something different or more of the same. Dilemma, they calls it."

"Healthy thirst, I calls it," said the elder Wilson son.

"I don't call it anything," said the other. "I just likes and enjoys it." Then as he finished his glass with a long sigh, he went on: "You know somethin'?"

"What?" asked his brother, wiping a white line of Guinness froth from his upper lip with his free hand.

"I just thought. Them cruises. They get up to all sorts of larks. Like what I mean, I read somewhere . . . well that the sea air goes to their heads and –"

"Ozone," said their father.

"What you mean?" asked the other brother.

"It's in the air," said his father. "Not like the air over the land, see. But sea air. It's full of ozone. Sort of turns people on. Like having one drink too many. Makes 'em fanciful. Romantic. You know what? She might come back engaged or something."

"You're daft."

"So I may be – but it's not your place as a son to put it so baldly."

"Why not – you're going a bit bald on top!"

At this the two sons fell about laughing and their father, a bottomless lake of tolerance, grinned and helped himself to the last of the Guinness.

Meanwhile their sister, Suzie Wilson, and Lily Franklin sat in the back of a hired car – driven by Joe Carter the self-employed owner, a round Tweedle-dee of a man with a habit of humming *sotto voce* as he drove the tunes from Gilbert and Sullivan operettas – on their way to Southampton.

Both girls were a little over-burdened by their controlled excitement, both holding themselves in so as not to seem less than adult to the other . . . both bubbling with inner excitement yet determined to preserve a ladylike demeanour and act as though it were far from the first time that they had been driven in state to Southampton to go off on a

45

Mediterranean cruise. But they were both far too natural to withold their true feelings for long.

It was Suzie Wilson who gave way first. As they drove through Marlborough on their way to Winchester she suddenly gave a deep sigh and flopping back against her seat said, "I got rats in the tummy about it all, Lily. What's it all going to be like? I mean . . . well, will we fit in? I mean first class. I've never been anywhere first class in my life. Except by mistake once and then the ticket collector turfed us out. You know what I mean? I seen the pictures in the brochure . . . everyone dressed for dinner and all that."

Maybe it was because Suzie had given way first that Lily Franklin – who felt much the same way as she did – found herself rising to the occasion and with an effort saying as calmly as she could, "Don't be silly, Sue. They're only people. And for all you know most of 'em will be the same as us. First time and rats in the tum until you really get going."

At this point Joe Carter, who could hear all they said, turned and grinned at them briefly and as his eyes went back to the road spoke over his shoulder, saying, "Don't you worry. Two nice girls like you. You'll have the time of your lives." Then he said in different tones, "Hullo . . . What's this then? Somebody in a spot of trouble, then?"

He braked slowly and came to a stop a few yards behind a saloon car that was drawn up at the roadside. Standing in its rear was a uniformed driver in a rosetted peaked cap and wearing a dark green chauffeur's outfit. Alongside the chauffeur was a young man in a grey flannel suit and wearing a black and white checked cap set very straight and prim on his head as though he was far from accustomed to the habit of wearing a cap or hat at all.

The driver came up to Joe and it was not possible for the two girls to hear what passed between them. In the meantime the young man – not really so young now, Suzie thought on having a good sight of him . . . maybe in his early thirties. Pleasant looking but a bit solemn-faced now, as he stood by while the two chauffeurs talked.

46

After a few moments Joe Carter turned and said, grinning, "Turn up for the book. This young gentleman's hired car's broken down. His driver wants to know if you'd give him a lift to the nearest garage where he can hire another car." Joe paused for a while, the grin lingering on his face and then went on, "I've told him that – with your permission – we can do better than that. We can take him all the way."

"All the way where?" asked Suzie Wilson.

The driver chuckled. "You'll never guess, miss."

"Then you'd better tell us," said Lily.

At this point the young man, who was clearly either embarrassed or of a very shy disposition, stepped forward to the rear of the car and said, "If you would kindly drop me at any garage you pass where I can hire a car I'd be very grateful. . . but, of course, if it's a bother to you . . . and there's all my baggage . . . two big cases. But they could go on your roof rack. I've got to get to Southampton by five o'clock. It's a Mediterranean cruise, and the ship – the *Andreas* – sails at six."

For a moment or two Suzie said nothing. Then she turned and looked at Lily and said, "Do you hear what he says?"

Lily giggled – which put a puzzled frown on the young man's brow – and then said, "I heard . . . Oh, I heard." They stared at one another and then collapsed in a fit of giggles.

The young man asked, "What is it so funny that I have said?" Just for a moment, even in her laughter fit, Lily fancied she could catch a slight foreign touch in the young man's voice.

Suzie, suddenly aware of their unintended rudeness, pulled herself together and with a very straight face said, "I'm sorry if we sound rude, but it's because of how it is. I mean, it's difficult to believe. You see – we're going to Southampton too. To go aboard the *Andreas* for a cruise."

"Really?"

"Really! Tell your driver to put your stuff on the luggage

47

rack with ours. And then you can sit up front. What's your name?"

"John Cristopher."

"John Christopher what?"

He smiled and the solemn, rather shy young man was suddenly gone, his face now alive and – she didn't know how to put it any better – the same but quite different . . . full of fun and a sort of calm happiness as though something good had happened to him. Well, and so it had, she thought. Not every breakdown brings a prompt rescue when you have to catch a boat or a train.

He said, "Just that – John Christopher. You sure this is no trouble to you? If you lifted me to the next town I could hire another car."

Lily shook her head and said, "Don't be daft, Mr Christopher. There's plenty of room. No point in wasting your money . . . After all we're all going to the same place."

"Well, I must say that it is a very fortunate thing for me. But you see . . . well, it's not that I'm not aware of how lucky it was that you came along but . . . well, I do think you should let me bear some of the cost because –"

Lily broke in sharply and said, "Now Mr Christopher – no more of that. It's our pleasure to be able to help you. But if you're going to be all upset about being given a free lift then I'll tell you what you can do – you can send a donation to some charity."

He smiled then and both girls were suddenly struck by the warmth and almost grinning pleasure that marked his expression . . . something of a small boy suddenly roused by a gift of a pleasing promise . . . and yet more than that . . . a sort of calmness behind his pleasure as though something had come right for him after a lot of doubt and uncertainty. He talked with an educated voice and was clearly – from the pigskin cases being lifted on to the roof rack by the two drivers – someone who had no lack of a bob or two.

As the young Mr Christopher supervised the storing of his cases and then stood settling up with his driver, Lily said, "I

48

think we've got a right one here. A bit la-de-dah and probably more money than sense. Funny thing – he reminds me of someone."

"Like who?"

"Dunno. No – like I seen him before, but couldn't have, could I?"

"Shouldn't think so. He's got nice eyes. Bluey-grey. Bit solemn 'cept when he smiles. Funny, going on the same cruise, isn't it?"

"Coincidence. That's what Mrs Ellington used to say."

"Used to say what?"

"That there weren't no such thing. It's all there waiting for us . . . you know like a film being shown. There it is – the future – all rolled up and ready to be shown. I dreamt about it last night, you know."

"About what?"

"About us going on this cruise and as I went aboard there was a young man with me – actually carrying my heavy hand grip. You know a nice sort of friendly helping hand and in his buttonhole he was wearing a pink sweet pea."

"What on earth's that got to do with anything?"

"Mrs Ellington, of course, and her language of flowers. I should know it by heart now. Sweet pea is for departure and lasting pleasure."

"What's that got to do with anything?"

"You've got eyes. Didn't you see what he was wearing in his buttonhole. A pink sweet pea."

"You mean you fancy him?"

"Oh, don't be so daft. You only think of one thing. There's umpteen sorts of pleasure in the world. I know there's lots of girls – and fellows, too – what have only got one thing on their mind. And then when they get married unless the whole thing's been right and proper and what the Fates intended . . . well, then repent at leisure."

"What are you talking about?"

"About what sweet peas mean. Delicate pleasures and departure. Well, isn't that like today. It's a pleasure to help

49

someone and we're all going on a departure. I tell you . . ." Lily gave a little sigh. "Nothing in this world happens by chance. Of course we think it does – but it doesn't. That's what religion's all about – but of course we don't get upset about it all being arranged in the future for us because, of course, we still don't know what it's going to be. So, in a way, it might not or need not be all arranged. Am I making myself clear?"

Suzie sighed. "I think so . . . Oh, dear. I suddenly remember I didn't do a thing about the laundry. And that lot won't do anything, of course. They'll just go on sleeping in the same old sheets. . . . Oh, dear. . . ."

At that moment the young man sitting in front with the driver turned and said, "Have you two young ladies brought sandwiches or anything like that for your lunch?"

Lily shook her head. "We thought we'd have a snack at some pub or café"

"Well, that would be nice. But I would be grateful if you would let me buy you lunch. After all . . . you are or have been a couple of helping angels to a traveller in trouble. Please do let me."

Suzie looked at Lily and they both smiled and Suzie said, "Well, that would be nice." And then, though she did not quite know why, except that his face was friendly and smiling and she could sense that he was a nice sort of fellow, she went on, "Have you been cruising before, Mr Christopher?"

"John. Please call me, John. And, yes, I have been before – but not very recently. And you?"

"No. Neither of us. We're a bit nervous about it, really, too. Also seasickness. Though we've got pills for that."

John Christopher studied them both with a mock frown on his face for a few seconds and then grinning said, "You don't have to worry. I can tell from people's faces, and I can promise you that neither of you will be seasick . . . whatever the weather."

"I don't see how you can be sure of that," said Lily.

"Well I am." He suddenly gave a wide, mischievous grin and said cockily, "I'm no ordinary chap. Oh, far from it. Full of surprises I am. Psychic and all sorts of things. If either of you have the slightest touch of *mal de mer* I'll eat my hat. You'll see."

"Well, I hope you're right," said Suzie. And then as she spoke she had the firm feeling that he would be. It was a feeling so strong that it not only surprised her but sent a swift little shiver racing down her backbone, like a gentle electric shock.

He grinned briefly and then composing his face, suddenly stern and really rather schoolmasterly and seeming older than he was, he said, "I am one of those people who is seldom if ever seriously wrong."

"Well," said Lily, "lucky you."

Breaking into a grin, he went on, "I know. I find it a great responsibility at times – do I speak or do I say nothing?"

A shade tartly, not sure how to assess his self confidence, Suzie said, "What about your responsibility for finding a nice place to eat, I'm starving."

He laughed then and said, "I do apologize. I've got a bad habit of talking too much and doing too little."

"Have you then?" said Suzie. "Well I'm used to that. I've got a father and three brothers who are all past masters of the art."

He laughed then and the sound was so infectious that the two girls laughed with him, but in the middle of her laughter, her eyes on the young man's face there suddenly came over Lily the odd but powerful feeling that she had seen him before. But for the life of her she could not think where or when . . . though she felt in the not-too-distant past. For a little while she pondered where she could have seen or met him, but if she had the memory escaped her . . . though at the back of her mind was the nagging feeling that it had not been so long ago and that . . . that . . . well that something had happened or something hadn't happened . . . oh, what was it? She puzzled for a while and then her attention was drawn

51

to what the stranger, leaning over his seat and talking to Suzie, was saying . . .

". . . nothing happens by accident really if you think about it – except of course the very first thing in creation which was the thought of it in God's mind. After that it's all been one tremendous great design being forever created like an endless ever-growing coloured tapestry, but one in which everything lives and grows and passes away only to return again in some other shape or combination of life and matter."

"Really . . ." said Suzie. "Well it's something to think about if you like that kind of thing. Personally I don't think it does any good to think too much about some things. Like why, for instance? Well, take the atomic bomb. That come of too much thinking and what good has that done or ever will do?"

Lily said, "I think the next nice-looking place we see we should have some lunch. I was too excited to eat much breakfast – but I'm really sharp-set now."

The young man laughed and said, "I like that. Sharp set. Oh, yes I like that. Well, we must find a place to blunt your sharp settedness, mustn't we?"

Suzie looked at Lily and raised her eyebrows and shoulders. Then with a grin at the young man, she said, "You mind if I ask you a question, a bit personal perhaps Mr Christopher?"

"John."

"John, then. What do you do for a living?"

"Of course I don't mind. I've done a lot of things – but just at the moment I'm in public relations. You know – people come to me with problems and I try and sort them out."

"What sort of problems?"

"Oh, usually family or personal affairs."

"Sometime you must come round to my family. You'd earn your money sorting them out."

"Maybe – but you know sometimes, quite unexpectedly,

52

people or families learn to sort themselves out . . . Yes, it happens. And it's the best way."

He laughed then and the sound was so infectious that the two girls laughed with him.

FOUR

THEY TOOK THE train from their local station to Charing Cross where, as Mrs Bell had warned him, a photographer and an interviewer from the woman's magazine met them and escorted them to as quiet a spot as they could find and took photographs of them for the magazine. Frank Langton submitted with good grace, grinning a little self-consciously since quite a few passers-by on the departure concourse stopped to see what was happening – hoping, no doubt, he thought, to spot some real celebrity and being disappointed. But anyway – the magazine wanted the pictures and there would possibly be more at Southampton . . . still, he could see that she was enjoying it all and – to be honest with himself – he wasn't feeling so awkward about it as he had thought he might be.

Just once the magazine representative, a young woman with blue eyes, a cherubic face and a soft manner which could suddenly turn sharp and incisive, confused him for a moment or two when she asked how long they had been engaged. Luckily, after a rather forced clearing of his throat he had said as calmly as he could manage, 'Oh, there's nothing like that. We're just very good friends. Old friends. Just that."

The interviewer in the hearing of them both had grinned and said, "Oh, a lot of people start out like that on a cruise and come back with the sound of wedding bells ringing in their ears not far off." And then, whether to spare him more embarrassment or because she genuinely wanted to know – though he couldn't think why, she went on, "Are you a good sailor? You know . . . seasickness?"

"It's never bothered me."

"And what are you looking forward to most of all?"

He was silent for a moment or two and then, a twinkle suddenly in his blue eyes and a grin on his face, he said, "To not having to get my own meals and washing up afterwards. Also making my bed and hoovering the sitting room carpet and –" he stopped and grinned, suddenly realizing that he was enjoying himself, thinking indeed that something was happening to him so that he felt lighter in body and spirit and unexpectedly really looking forward to the change that was coming over his life. He resumed, "A complete change in –" he turned and with a slight but gallant inclination of his head – which the attendant photographer got – said, "the best company in the world I could ever have hoped for."

The girl interviewer laughed then and said, "You ought to write romantic fiction. Well . . . both of you . . . have the time of your lives."

"We shall do our best," said Mrs Bell and as the interviewer left them she said to him, "Sorry about that. It's all a bit cheeky, but I suppose –"

Interrupting her he said, "Oh, that's all right, Nancy dear. She's got her job to do for the magazine. And anyway, she was quite nice about it. After all, you know, the people who read the magazine want to know all about you – and I suppose me. They put themselves in our place and do a little daydreaming. So we shouldn't mind."

She put out a hand and touched his arm, smiling, and said, "Of course." She then gave a little laugh and, with a sudden hint of almost diffidence, despite the years they had known one another, she went on, "You know . . . it's a funny thing. All these years we've got used to one another but now . . . well, but now . . ."

"But now – what?"

"Well, it'll sound daft. But it's like we haven't known one another for very long and . . . well, we're a bit shy of one another. At least something like that. Like as though we were

55

two different people and that we've left our old selves back home in Castleport."

"Well, perhaps that's what we have done. Perhaps that's what the gods or the fates or whatever are playing at. Stirring us up a bit. I do feel that. Kind of a new man or . . . well, being given a last chance before settling into being a real old oldie with little more than meals on wheels to look forward to. Don't you feel like that, Nancy? If you're not careful you can slowly let yourself be older than you really are. Sixty is nothing these days. There's a chap at the golf club does eighteen holes every other day regularly and he's well over eighty. In fact –" he gave a short laugh "– chaps at the club say that he's been up to ninety and now he's gone into reverse and he's looking forward to his second fiftieth birthday."

She laughed and said, "I like you a lot when you are like that. Suddenly all full of confidence . . . sort of strong and being leaderlike. Nothing any trouble. I can see you as an army man . . . a leader. Well, that's all right with me." She gave him a big smile, and added, "From now on, you're in charge. You give the orders and I obey."

"Obey?"

"Yes. What you say goes . . . unless of course –"

"It doesn't suit your book?"

"Perhaps." She took his arm, giving him a little tug, said, "Come on, we've got a boat train to catch from Water-loo . . ."

"No problem," he said.

And as though the gods would have him proved right and perhaps by so doing indicate interest in their affairs a porter materialized with a hand trolley and took charge of their luggage and led them away to find a taxi which would take them to Waterloo Station and so to their boat train for the journey to the dockside at Southampton where the S.S. *Andreas* waited for the coming of her cruise passengers.

A little later they were sitting in the train at a small window table for two . . . at the moment Mrs Bell and, indeed, Frank Langton (though neither of them had said so to the other) wanted to be free of other people and the need to make or sustain conversation. They were together, alone, starting on . . . what? thought Mrs Bell – an adventure, perhaps even, in a way, a new phase of their lives. Oh, yes, she told herself – and not for the first time that day – sometimes you could feel that a day was different from all others, that it was going to lead to something . . . to something different. Whether it would be something pleasant or disappointing . . . well, a lot of that usually depended on yourself.

Looking round the coach Frank Langton was free of any thought of things being different. In a curious way – though he had known this before in himself – he was neither excited nor indifferent about the coming holiday. He was holding himself in reserve and also keeping a watchful eye on himself since now he was not travelling alone, but, whether she accepted it or not, had the responsibility of ushering and looking after Nancy. Oh, yes – they had from their first good-morning after the evening when he had gone to the church, dropped into a first-name habit without comment . . . after all those years. No, at the moment he was keeping himself free of any over emotion. The regiment, as it were, was on the move . . . and he was in charge. When they had had their photographs taken at Charing Cross and the girl interviewer had asked him about his war years for a moment he had been tempted to go into his over-coloured version but then, feeling Nancy's hand on his arm as they stood together, he had said, "Oh, nothing exciting ever happened to me. I was one of the lucky ones, I suppose."

Sitting opposite him Nancy, as the train pulled out of the station, was to her own surprise suddenly seized with emotion which she could not entirely hide. She reached across the small table and took one of his large, strong hands and said, "Now we're on our way . . . no more interviews or anything like that. Just us. Like any other couple." She gave him a big smile, and went on, "You really are pleased about it all, Frank? Not just . . . well being good-natured and wanting to please me? But happy for yourself, too? Like it's a fairy godmother gift. Something neither of us could have really afforded on our own."

He was silent for a moment, gently smiling at her and then, indifferent as to who might see him doing it in this public carriage he raised her hand to his lips and kissed it briefly, but still holding it said, "Of course I am. It's so good that I almost have to really pinch myself now and again to make sure I'm not just dreaming it . . ."

Perhaps very few of the other people in the long coach saw the intimate gesture, or, if they did, were touched and understanding because it also stirred something in their own hearts at that moment . . . happiness, slowly growing excitement, a dream minute by minute becoming a reality worked through the carriage like some invisible elixir which few failed to be sensible of though they might have been hard put to explain it in adequate words.

James Goodbody saw the gesture as he came into the carriage. He had a seat in a coach three ahead of this one and – as was always his habit when he went on a cruise – he liked to travel to the port with the bulk of the passengers and, once aboard the cruise train, he liked to take a stroll through a few of the carriages so that he could size up the company he would be moving among. Sometimes – he had a sense of humour with many sides – he called it looking over the prospects . . . his prospects. All these people, sitting dressed for rail travel . . . sober suits and best costumes or casual dress over which much time had been spent . . . human beings with all their quirks and dreams and – no matter how many times they had done it before – with excitement enlivening them at the prospect of being on shipboard . . . of the splendid and luxurious isolation with others on a floating paradise where (for James Goodbody was a well-read young man, whatever his morals might be) every prospect was pleasing and only man was vile. And – sadly but long accepted by him – he was perhaps a little viler than most of

them – but not in any brutal, physically harming way. No
. . . savages used wooden clubs – but gentlemen used the
sword . . . the rapier. And no matter how far down in the
world the Goodbody family had eventually come (and he
one of only a widely dispersed handful of survivors) –
whatever he did he did with politeness and charm and, of
course, the utmost skill and expertise if it were anything to do
with cards or gambling. He and the odds of chance were old
and inseparable friends. Twice a year he took a cruise to
bring a change from what he called his 'landside work' – the
races and gambling clubs. Any card game you could name
and he had it at his fingertips and the odds of chance and
coincidence came naturally almost to him.

Seeing Frank's gesture he was briefly touched, for there
was such an old-fashioned elegance about it, and elegance
was something that he sought and admired above almost
everything. Whatever you do it is not enough to do it well: do
it with style . . . panache . . . grace . . . lose like a gentleman
. . . rob like one too . . . be a cultured highwayman not a
ragged-arsed foot-pad. He smiled at the thought and the
memory it brought. No father's words – for he had never
known one – but his mother's (alas, now long and too soon
dead) and one of the greatest card players he had ever met
. . . a genius far outreaching his own considerable skills and
expertise – though she claimed even she could not match her
late husband's gambling skill.

Now he was off for another cruise and he had long since
ceased to remember with exactitude the number of cruises he
had made . . . long, short, profitable or just paying off. And –
his face went sombre, the sparkle in his eyes was muted as his
inward grimace of self pity was reflected outwardly – he
knew now that he had had more than enough of them. As the
old song said, "he had ranged and roamed in his time". No –
with a grimace, remembering the exactitude of his scholarly
and much-loved and disreputable mother – never mind
about "a woman being only a woman but a good cigar is a
smoke" Or was he right. . . ? These days – perhaps he was

getting woolly minded, although his skill at cards was unblemished – he did get his memories a bit mixed. Well, why not? He might look early thirties . . . raven-black hair, blue eyes (unusual), slim, athletic body – this from squash and early morning runs, an addiction, perhaps also a form of worship for, being an atheist, he warmed himself with a little daily self-worship – which he called "keeping in trim" – and this not so easy for him, since his mode of life was far from that of being the early bird. More often than not he went to bed as the first morning bird calls rang out sleepily from Regent's Park.

Looking round the carriage he saw no one he had seen before on cruises, but he knew perfectly well that when he got aboard there would be three or four at least almost well enough known to be called old acquaintances and to make a quorum of night lovers of the green baize table and the spinning roulette wheel. But never a penny again on a horse. "The most unreliable of creatures" . . . he grinned, remembering his mother's words. What a pair his parents had been! Deeply in love from the moment they had met and both devout worshippers at the high altar of Chance. Now if he could only meet someone like his mother . . . well, then he might be tempted to make his final oblations to the goddess who ruled all men's lives and forsake for ever one of her main attractions . . . perhaps. He grinned to himself openly and, as he did so, three seats farther up the carriage a young woman sitting on the outside of the double seat caught his eye and out of some instant sympathetic happiness or embarrassment at the pleasure on his face, smiled back at him so that out of devilment he added a quick wink to his smile and then lifted his evening paper and hid behind it to save her further embarrassment. But that did not hide her face. A man with a true card memory never forgets a face. To do so might be costly at some time. Nice girl though, he thought; then sighed, shook open his evening paper as he felt the movement of the train begin and the platform began to slide away behind him. Here we go, he thought. And wryly –

remembering his mother – down to the sea in chips . . . and counters and crumpled notes . . . and odds and chances and mathematical probabilities and pretty girls all in a row. The time was getting near when he would have to pick one and – seriously, no half-measures – start all the love, honour and obey business. No, that was what she had to do. And as his mother would have said, no mucking about with newfangled rituals . . . let it be – *I take thee* (whoever it is) *to my wedded husband, to have and to hold from this day forward, for better for worse for richer for poorer, in sickness and in health, to love, cherish and to obey, till death us do part, according to God's holy ordinance: and thereto I give thee my troth* . . . And no damn modern nonsense. *With my body I thee worship, and* – important but far from incompatible this – *with all my worldly goods I thee endow* . . .

My God, he thought . . . my old man loved the cards and the green baize, the roulette wheel and the horses. He lived by skill and chance and the greatest of these (mother had said, he used to say) is nothing against a clear conscience, a prompt payment of bills when possible and if a beggar puts out a hand never spurn it. Give and do it *ex mero motu* and, since your Latin (she would say) is and always will be lousy, that means *of one's own unrestrained impulse*; and apparently he always did as he said. Though that was by no means the reason he died practically penniless. Ah, well . . . that was something that was never going to happen to *him*.

He smiled to himself and was suddenly aware that the train was moving smoothly away from the platform.

Here we go, he thought. Like the old song. *Just one more time . . . just one more chance* . . . Well, he would like to think it would be – though the good Lord knew what he would do without the cards, the green baize, the spinning wheel and, even if pushed, bingo.

He lay back and closed his eyes and the girl a few seats back who had smiled at him, though she had no idea why, saw that his dark hair was thinning and told herself that he was probably the type that went bald early. Then, other thoughts crowding in, she turned to her mother sitting beside her and said, "He looked nice, didn't he?"

"Who?"

"That chap up there who turned round and looked back at us. The one by himself. You can just see the top of his head – he's settling down for a sleep."

"I can see the top of his head, and he's going thin there. He'll be bald by the time he's forty odd. Not like your dear departed father – you should have seen the head of hair he had as a young man. Lovely blond hair. Norwegian blood I always say he had. That's where you get yours. Well, keep your fingers crossed. Perhaps this time we'll have better luck and Mr Right will be aboard."

* * * *

At the dockside in the great departure shed they were separated from their cabin luggage which was taken aboard the S.S. *Andreas* lying alongside . . . a towering leviathan rising sheer above the quayside, gleaming with white paint, smoke gently wafting from its twin after funnels. Unable yet to go through Customs and on to the quayside, passengers gathered in the great hall, filling the few available seats, while others perched on their hand luggage or strolled up and down in a restless promenade. Outside, alongside the quay, lay the S.S. *Andreas*. Crew, porters and others, went up and down the gangway while the congregation of passengers in the wharf shed grew and a ragged queue began to form itself, shifting from foot to foot, waiting for Customs to open and boarding to begin.

And in this period of waiting some disintegration of temporary groups arose. The young man, John Christopher, after again thanking Lily and Suzie for the lift they had given him – and they for the lunch to which he had treated them – drifted away, carefree now without more than hand baggage to cope with and it was a good fifteen minutes before they realized that he had gone.

62

"No great loss," said Lily. "Not that I didn't like him – but I don't think he would have been much fun. Sort of serious in a quiet way, weren't he?"

"Withdrawn," said Suzie.

"What do you mean?"

"Nice and polite – but something on his mind. Not quite with us. A gent, though – but not much good I'd say at a *Knees up, Mother Brown*. Intellectual, I'd say. Half in this world and half in some other. He's either a poet or he's got a bit missing somewhere."

"Well, one thing he hasn't got missing is cash. That was a really good lunch and I saw his wallet when he paid. Stuffed."

"You can't tell with people, can you," said Suzie. "Look at this lot –" she waved a hand around the growing crowd and queue in the shed and said, "Pick 'em up and put 'em in Marks and Spencers now and nobody would think any of them a bit odd. Just people – not really dressed up at all."

"People don't these days."

"Don't what? Dress up for travelling."

"Yes. It's the Welfare State. We're all rich and we're all happy, and we don't have to prove anything by the clothes we wear – not travelling, anyway." Lily gave a giggle and said, "I'm glad I went when we had lunch."

"What do you mean?"

"Made myself comfortable. There's only a small place out back with a queue a mile long. It's waiting what does it."

Suzie said, "I hope you aren't going to talk like that when we get aboard."

"Course not. Don't worry, I can mind my . . . oh, dear." She giggled and burst into laughter.

"Now what's the matter?" asked Suzie.

Lily contained herself and said, straight-faced, "I was going to say – Can mind my pees and queues."

*   *   *   *

63

On the promenade deck Suzie and Lily, just two amongst the passengers who lined the rail, waiting for the ship to move away from the dockside, listened to the music coming from the band of the 16th/5th Queen's Royal Lancers on the quay below them. They had already found their cabin and left their hand luggage there, but their two heavy suitcases had yet to be delivered.

When they had entered the cabin and had a good look round . . . bathroom and lavatory, a fitted dressing table, plenty of drawer space and a hanging cupboard for clothes and a radio . . . they had both felt much of their nervous anticipation begin to fade. They were home . . . or what they were to call home for a long time . . . this was their refuge, their own place for as long as they were aboard and Suzie had suddenly said, "You know – it's suddenly all gone. And that makes a lot of difference."

"What does?"

"That sort of rats in the tummy feeling. What's it going to be like feeling and always eating in a posh restaurant and what will the others at the table be like. Isn't it like that with you when you do something new. I mean, think: we're going to have to sit at a table in the restaurant with four or five people we don't know from Adam. But now . . . now that I'm here – it's all gone. I feel happy and without any cares to bother about. I don't mind if those damned men of mine set the house afire. I shan't be there to worry about it. What I mean is – I'm me without any strings or fussations. Don't you feel that?"

"Yes, I suppose I do – but perhaps not as strong as you because I don't have any father and brothers to be glad to see the back of me. There's only Aunt Rachel and we've always got along."

"Well, you've been lucky in a way. But it takes all sorts, don't it? You're used to a nice quiet sort of life with your aunt. But I don't think that would suit me. My lot drive me mad sometimes. But they're all good at heart and I know that if I was in trouble they'd rally round. There was this

64

bloke who began to pester me a bit when I went down to the shopping centre – nothing really out of order, but a nuisance. Dad and the lads waited for him after the shop closed and took him for a drink. Ever so polite they were, they said, and treated him to a couple of whiskies and the benefit of their advice. He dives out into the storeroom at the back any time I go into the shop now . . . Oh, Lord—"

"Now what?"

"Well everything. But just now . . . well, going down to dinner and meeting the others at the table."

Suzie laughed and said, "You're a good one. Making trouble for yourself beforehand. Don't be stupid. They'll just be people and, maybe, most of them feeling just as you do now. So forget it. Only thing I'm not sure about is what table we go to."

Quite suddenly Lily had been annoyed with herself, though she showed nothing of this to Suzie. She was here because she had been good to Mrs Ellington – and Mrs Ellington – a decidedly forthright person – wouldn't have stood for any nonsense of 'wondering this and that'. People were people – like liquorice allsorts they came in different sizes and colours and shapes – but fundamentally they were all more or less the same – give or take a bit. She was here with her good friend Suzie and they were going to enjoy themselves.

The band below began to play 'The Road to the Isles' – or at least that was what Suzie thought it was but she hadn't got much of a memory for music and songs. She was a hummer, filling in the gaps between the bits she remembered with her own *da-da-de-da-da-di-das* and from somewhere on the crowded decks of the S.S. *Andreas* coloured streamers were thrown, snaking brilliantly through the air to be caught by the quayside crowd and held as the restraining hawsers were slipped from their bollards, and suddenly it seemed there was a steadily increasing gap between ship and shore.

Then from behind her a familiar voice said, "It's always a sad moment, isn't it – although it's a happy one. Funny that

65

– how joy and sadness so often go together. Sad to go. Happy to be going."

She turned to see John Christopher standing behind her. He was smiling, the slight shore breeze gently ruffling his hair and he was wearing a small sprig of white sweet pea flowers in his buttonhole.

Without knowing why she did it she reached forward and touched the flowers and said, "They are good flowers to wear. They stand for departure and lasting pleasure. Do you think we shall have that?"

He said, "I don't see why not. We're departing already. Lasting pleasure . . . well, that's always there. It just is that a lot of people don't understand that no matter what happens to them that life is a lasting pleasure . . . like faith."

"You should preach a sermon about it."

He laughed. "Not for me . . . Oh, no – not for me. I'm too busy doing other things."

"Like what, if I may ask?"

"Working for my father."

"At what?"

"Public relationships."

"Sounds dull."

"It sometimes is . . . Now look –" he turned slowly and pointing said, "We're clearing the docks. Soon we'll see the Needles at the end of the Isle of Wight and then we'll be in the Channel – really at sea. That's the time people begin to think about being seasick . . . doesn't matter if there's only a tiny little swell going they find they suddenly feel whoozy and a little off balance and they hurry to their bunks."

Suzie said, "Do you have to spell it out? You're making me feel funny already."

He laughed. "Oh, no – that's excitement. I've been sea travelling long enough to spot the types who do and those who don't."

"Do and don't do what?"

"Get seasick. It's all in the mind you see."

"So what's in my mind?"

66

He grinned. "Gladness and happiness and a tiny touch of nervousness. But you won't be seasick. You don't have the aura – either of you."

"What's an aura?" asked Suzie.

"Your spiritual emanation."

"Come again. Emanation?"

Lily said, "The kind of waves you give off or sometimes like a kind of light all around you? Mrs Ellington was a great believer in it. She always said mine was pale primrose colour."

"Sounds daft to me," said Suzie. "That would mean you would have to be careful what colour dress you wore to match your . . . well, whatever it was."

John Christopher laughed and said, "No – there's no trouble there. You see if you've got a good aura it automatically changes colour to match mood, dress and thoughts."

"Pull the other," said Suzie, and then after he had left them with a little bob of his head and the suggestion of a bow, she said to Lily, "What do you make of him? You think he's got a screw loose?"

"I don't know – but he's been very kind to us, remember."

"That's true."

*   *   *   *

It had been easy, of course, to find out the name of the young woman on the boat train with – he presumed – her mother. On the rack above their seats had been stacked two small overnight cases, both of them labelled with an official cruise label. He got up and walked back to the toilet and then on his return pretended to sway with the motion of the train and put up a hand to the luggage rack rail and read the official cruise labels – Mrs and Miss Picton, and the cabin number which he knew from experience was an outside double-berth cabin on 'A' deck . . . a choice far out of his reach normally – though there had been short periods in his

67

life when the cards had fallen well for him and the wheel had turned in his favour and the horses had run for him, when he had known brief periods of temporary affluence which had whetted and sustained his ambition for a more permanent indulgence from the goddess of fortune. And why not? He was an honest man. He merely took chances, calculated the odds against or for, was liberal with his winnings and philosophical with any untoward loss, and more than this – he knew that he was his own worst enemy because he had other abilities . . . a first-class brain, a pleasant but never overdone social manner, a good education and an appreciation of literature and the arts and an ability to play the piano with some little distinction and to sing in a light baritone which would have been welcomed in any end-of-pier concert party . . . But he was love's victim . . . a devotee of the Lady of Chance. And something told him that he always would be until some woman of beauty and reasonable fortune fell for him, married him and so set him free to do the only thing in the world which ranked higher in his affections than Lady Luck – and that was to own and run a small nursery or garden centre outside some pleasant town . . . damned silly, of course, but there it was, firmly planted in his mind and he was stuck with it. Sometimes he even hoped that he could make it come true and then find it had all been totally wrong – that he would fast become sick and tired of plants and pricking-out and potting-up and knowing that half the plants he sold would die within a few months because the purchasers would neglect them. Ah, well, in the meantime there was always this . . . the pleasures of the chase and the final despoiling of the victim. Though, of course, this was always done with courtesy – so many men sitting to the green baize table were just geese come to market to be plucked . . . Um, something a bit wrong with the analogy there, he told himself, but at least he knew what was in his mind, even if he couldn't get the right words for it.

Now, some hours later, he sat in his single outside cabin on 'B' deck, starboard side, his prone body moving gently to the

68

motion of the ship, and told himself that it was time that he got ready to go down to dinner – first sitting – and to face the pleasure or boredom or a mixture of both which would be presented by the other passengers at his table. Unless you had made a prior arrangement with the restaurant manager about a table – some couples or foursomes liked a table to themselves . . . the more gregarious just took what came, and some had a definite preference for a large table . . . eight or ten people, plenty of company, plenty of talk. For himself he just took what came so long as it was a large table. People were his business. The more he met the more . . . well, the more the chances of . . . well, let it be said, improving one's chance of making desirable contact.

Not entirely to his surprise the restaurant manager as he entered recognized him and said, "Welcome back again, Mr Goodbody. Nice to have you aboard."

He grinned. "Good Lord – you've got a good memory. It was a couple of years ago."

"Well, some faces stick and others don't – but with you it was the card room late one night. I was off duty and walked in and saw you dealing. You ever fly-fish?"

"No."

"Well – you can always tell one who has the touch and the skill. Everything made to look so easy. Poetry . . . all lovely motion. Same with cards and a man's hands." He grinned widely, and added, "Cards, fly rods, and handling dogs and horses . . . there's always the caressing under the commanding."

Goodbody smiled. "You're wasted down here. We should go into partnership. You analyse the characters and I operate on them. Bluffable, unbluffable . . . two drinks and rash . . . five drinks and head like iron . . . and as for women. Well – though they're more unpredictable – if we got them right there's more money in it. Interest you?"

"No, thanks. Though I appreciate the compliment – but I'm happy as I am . . . well, most of the time anyway. What was our last run together?"

69

"Norwegian fiords. Land of the Midnight Sun."

"Ah, yes. Well, I've put you at an interesting table. But no green baize or *rouge et noir* boys amongst them."

"Thank God."

"So, enjoy your fillet of plaice, bonne femme and roast guinea fowl."

"Served in burgundy sauce?"

"Of course. And since you once did me a very good turn I've told them to let you have a bottle of vintage Château St-Bonnet any time you ask for it. Which I imagine you will some time when you are dining *à deux?*"

"Could be."

"Bon appétit, m'sieur."

He moved to his table, led by a steward who had taken his table number, took a quick glance round at his companions as he stood by the chair which the steward was holding, and said, "I'm James Goodbody. Good evening to you all."

At this the young man John Christopher stood up, metaphorically adjusting the mantle of command comfortably about his shoulders, and said, "Welcome to table number seven, Mr Goodbody. Now let me introduce you to your fellow travellers and table companions – and if I get the names not quite right. Well . . . I know I'll be forgiven."

Whereupon as Goodbody stood and John Christopher made the introductions . . . a nod and smile for each one . . . the memory bank which was Goodbody's mind took them all in – the names committed faultlessly to memory, and then to each one a small comment . . . a point of reference which, triggered in the computer of his brain, would come up at instant command. Though as the introductions were finished and he sat down, a stab of disappointment came as he saw at the adjacent six-seater table Mrs and Miss Picton and – the impulse rising unexpectedly and uncharacteristically, for he detested all forms of vulgarity or forwardness – as the young lady looked in his direction he gave her a quick wink and knew at once that it had not been unwelcome, since her face for a moment or two showed no

70

change and then a slow smile took her lips and she lowered her head, as though bashful and not wanting him to see her obvious welcoming interest . . . or at least, that was what he hoped it was.

As he sat down the table waiter came to him, handing him the elaborate menu. He studied it carefully, since he gave to his food all the thought which he knew it deserved. Whatever he did he did with care and forethought, not in any way fussing but giving due weight and respect to the by-no-means least considerable of mankind's activities. It was not enough to eat to live – stolen turnips and a snared rabbit would provide that – but fine food came from the gods – one of the consolations to man for the lack of life eternal. When I die (he used to muse in his more unsober moments) let it be after a good dinner of, say, Parma ham with melon, skip the soup, fillet of halibut Bercy . . . ah, that white wine and parsley sauce . . . skip the entrée and go straight to a sirloin steak *au poivre* with green peas and French fried potatoes and then, perhaps, a méringue Chantilly and skip the cheese for fresh fruit . . . Château Latour with the steak, to be preceded by a Bourgogne Aligoté with the halibut . . . lovely – and he nodded understandingly and quite convincingly to the person on his right who was talking to him while his eyes looked beyond the confines of his table to the adjacent one where the young lady of the boat train had too obviously casually turned to look at him. Good class, he told himself. Plenty of money – how fortunate some people were! Too often, though, good things of life were in the wrong hands.

At that moment the voice at his side said, "You've been cruising many times, Mr Goodbody?"

"Too many times I sometimes think, Mr Christopher."

"Why do you say that?"

"Because I don't do it just for pleasure like most people, Mr Christopher. You see –"

He stopped speaking and after a moment or two gave the other a grin and shrugged his shoulders.

Mr Christopher said, "Why don't you call me John?"

"I will but not for a while. I like to come to things slowly. I don't mean to be rude but there's something about being at sea that makes people, I think, too quickly free and easy. Perhaps it's the air. Or perhaps I'm prejudiced. You see I come cruising for quite a diff–" He broke off abruptly, aware, and surprised, that he had almost unthinkingly been going to speak a truth that after all these years he still found somewhat shaming . . . that for him this was not nor had been so many others, just a pleasure cruise. This was a once-a-year holiday with work. There had not been a single cruise yet which had not seen him at its end very much richer in pocket than he had been when he went aboard. No question of dishonesty or cheating, mind you. No, just that he had the memory and the brain which together turned him into a highly primed calculating machine which took facts and the factors of odds and evens and chances and which, faithfully followed or obeyed, gave him rewards which almost consistently outpaced his losses. Add to that the small income from a family trust whose capital he could not touch until he was forty and he managed to get by quite comfortably, though not in luxury.

Mr Christopher said, "I know why you come. I guess you're like me. I have what I call an appetite for people." He laughed briefly. "Not cannibalistic. But just for being with people . . . new people once or twice a year. You've cruised before a lot, haven't you?"

"Yes. Work and pleasure. It's O.K. now at my age. But I don't think I'm going to fancy it when I'm old and grey."

"I don't think you need worry."

"Well, I hope you're right. Nice wife, steady income from wise investments and a house in some pleasant village. Something like that."

At this moment the steward came to his side and asked him for his dinner order, and as he gave it he found himself wondering with surprise that he had talked so openly about a wife, investment income and a nice village house to his dinner neighbour. These were all part of his dream of the

future and strictly not to be shared with anyone else. Ah, well
. . . perhaps now and again it was all right. Still . . . He gave
a quick sideways glance at Mr Christopher and wondered
what it was about him that roused – he couldn't say excited –
his interest. But there was something odd about the man . . .
young man, really. What? Mid-thirties at the most.

Then something happened which drove all other thoughts
from his mind. From the next table the young lady of the
boat train turned her head slowly and looked at him, her face
solemn, almost severe, and she seemed to become frozen in
her poise . . . almost, he thought, as though she were under
some spell. Then, most astonishingly, she closed and opened
her right eye slowly in a long wink.

He was so amazed that he had a momentary near
complete loss of breath and had to brace himself to take air
into his lungs. The thing was impossible . . . marvellous . . .
it was – years of doing crosswords paid off at last – a
serendipity that left him feeling slightly giddy as he quickly
made a brief inclination of his head in acknowledgement.

She turned away and he lowered his eyes (having already
refused from the extensive menu fruit juices, appetisers and
soups) to his river trout meunière normande . . . cooked in
butter, and garnished with shrimps and mushrooms. Slowly,
holding down his excitement, he ate a few of the garnishing
shrimps and mushrooms, and breathed deeply, thinking to
himself, the thought a recurring but gentle drumbeat . . .
How could it be? How could it be? Never in his life before had
he been so taken . . . so up-lifted . . . so smitten. Here must be
the beginning of a miracle . . . and his feet, if the gods were
good, at last on the road to . . . No, he would not be arrogant
enough to say eternal happiness but the road to . . .
happiness and, surely, freedom from want and from the
green baize cloth?

After the first sitting of diners was over there followed the
nightly cabaret-type entertainment – one of which followed
each of the two dinner sittings taking place in the Paradise
Room at the stern of the promenade deck. Everyone at the

73

table went to watch it, many of them carrying off with them –
an acceptable custom – their individual dinner menu which
that evening had a coloured cover illustration of a pair of
goldfinches – *carduelis carduelis* which probably in some way,
so John Christopher had informed them, came from their
fondness for eating thistle head seeds – the Latin name for a
thistle being *carduus* – which had made Lily Franklin sitting
next to Suzie whisper to her, "Well, the common thistle
stands for austerity. None of that around here at the
moment, is there? Mind you, if it were a Scotch thistle that
would be for retaliation, and I can't see any place for that
around either, can you? What would we retaliate at or for?
Everything's lovely."

Suzie cocked an eye at her and whispered, "You don't 'ave
no more after you've finished that glass. You got to come to
wine slowly if you're not used to it. He's a bit of a rum 'un,
ain't he?"

"Who?"

"Christopher John . . . no, John Christopher. How can
you have two Christian names and no proper surname?
Though, come to think of it, I had a friend at school who had
a brother called Arthur George. You see their surname
was –"

"Yes, I see, Suzie . . ."

FIVE

SITTING IN THE Neptune Room, which was at the after end of the promenade deck and quite close to the ship's library, Mrs Richard Chambers was reading, or appearing to be reading, the book which she had just borrowed. She had had a long day, and a day full of movement and change so that it was restful now to sit down with an open book on her lap – perhaps not to be read just yet but certainly a token that she did not wish to be drawn into conversation . . . not that that was likely, but one can never know situations in this world. A good-looking, pleasant woman, she kept her eyes on the open book but did no reading. The book was her shield. Behind it lay herself and her world, not the world of this ship, but of the small country town where she had been born, educated, married and suffered humiliation without being able to summon up the spirit to retaliate in any satisfactory way.

Just at this moment, had she the magic power, she knew that if it were possible she would never go back to England. If she had a fortune of her own, enough money to live a life of comfort anywhere she chose, she knew that she would never go back to her home town . . . and the flat . . . and to her husband. In fact, even having money of her own wouldn't be necessary. She could get a job and live with her brother . . . a divorce, even. Tears faintly misted her eyes as she thought of the early days of meeting with Richard. . . . He'd been a different person then – jolly, caring, all over her with treats, trips to London, theatres, dances and – which she cared for most of all – the days when they both got on their bicycles

75

and explored the country far and wide. She'd lived then as though she were floating through life, which was like a fairytale come true . . . well, something like that. Then after a few years of married life – hard ones, for he had opened another sweets-and-tobacco shop and business everywhere was slumping – he had changed. Oh, how often had she searched her memory and severely cross-examined herself and her conscience, wondering if she were at all to blame . . . wondering whether she gave him too little support . . . sympathy or understanding – but in all truth could not see that she could take blame for the change in him. And now . . . it was all over. He would, she knew, eventually divorce her . . . but she would never have divorced him. Her belief was an unalterable part of her life . . . *Wilt thou obey him, and serve him, love, honour, and keep him in sickness and in health; and, forsaking all other, keep thee only unto him, so long as ye both shall live*? If one made a promise before God – then the promise had to be kept. But he had left her and so denied her the simple rights to which they had both sworn.

For a moment or two she felt the faint prick of held tears in her eyes and taking her handkerchief from her handbag she gave her nose a good blow to cover her emotion. As she did so John Christopher came towards her from the far end of the Neptune Room, where there was a small bar. He carried a glass in each hand, gave her a smile as he approached and then sat down at her little table and placed a glass in front of her and his own he cradled in both hands; she saw that it was a small brandy balloon glass.

He gave her a mock admonitory shake of his head and said, "You looked so all alone – though, of course, not palely loitering – that I thought you needed cheering up. That's a Grand Marnier."

She smiled, cheered by his pleasant company and said, "How did you know I liked Grand Marnier?"

"Well . . ." he laughed gently, ". . . it's a thing I've got. Often I seem to know things about people – even people I've

76

never met before. It's like that feeling you get sometimes when you turn into a strange street or drive into a village, or that kind of thing which happens with people, too, when you say to yourself, *I've been here before* or *All this has happened to me before*. I just knew you were a Grand Marnier woman."

"Do you mean that you're psychic?"

"Indeed not. And such an overworked word with all its derivatives. Psyche just means a butterfly and in Greek mythology the personification of the soul . . . which was usually shown as a young woman with butterfly wings with whom Eros fell in love. Words are beautiful things – but behind them all lie great mysteries and sometimes great dangers. Now tell me – and forgive my curiosity – why do you prefer to sit alone? Your brother, is it, in ship's uniform I've seen talking to you from time to time? Are you travelling with anyone else?"

"I think, and I mean it without offence, I'd rather not talk about that. Suffice to say I am travelling alone, and – yes – the man who talks to me in uniform is my brother John Eggerton, who arranged the trip for me."

"Then I will tell you something. I know you may not believe this – and I don't make it known to many people. But to those who know, or feel that there are more things –"

"In heaven and earth than are dreamt of in your philosophy, Horatio?"

He laughed, and said. "Yes. Well, to come to the point: I can tell you that . . . when you get back from this cruise it will mean for you the beginning of one of the happiest, but in some ways the saddest, parts of your life . . . but also a way of living which will give you great and deep satisfaction."

"Oh, really. How can you possibly know this?"

"How does a shepherd looking over his flock know – without counting – that one is missing? How do you know by looking at some men or women that they are not to be trusted? And others you would put your life in their hands without qualms? Trust is a virtue that those in need recognize in others at once. Now –" he gave her a big smile –

77

"I suggest that you let me escort you into the Albatross Room, where I hope you will have the courage to dance with me. I've always been told that I was born with two left feet."

She laughed, feeling suddenly full of well being and said, "I think you're one of those who hide their light under a bushel."

He laughed and said, "I've always thought that comprised a dangerous fire risk."

She smiled at him as they took the floor and as they danced on she had the feeling growing strong in her that this John Christopher really did have something which other men lacked . . . something odd . . . something elusive and yet really something very simple to spot if only one's memory could reach back. That was it. Somewhere in her memory he existed already. And at this she shook with frustration that she could not recall when or where. Perhaps because of her frustration she lost some of her natural reticence and sense of decorum . . . for a moment or two she was roused by the still sharp memories of her husband . . . and oddly she had a vivid sensation that she had seen this John Christopher before, although she could summon up no clear memory of where or when.

When they sat at their table at the finish of a waltz — during which she had told him where she came from and what her husband did, though she suppressed any mention of the distress he had and was still causing her — she said "And may I ask what you do for a living, Mr Christopher?"

"Of course." He smiled and by some trick of light she saw herself reflected in his eyes . . . herself . . . two tiny figures, dwarfed and remote. "Of course, you may. I work for my father. We have a very, very big organization. I couldn't go into the details of his many enterprises but I . . . well, I'm a cross between a publicity man and a salesman. Not that we sell any actual goods . . . like typewriters or motor cars . . . no, we specialize in ideas and management consultancy."

"And you like it?"

"Oh, very much. But it's sometimes disappointing work.

78

One fails." He grinned suddenly, appearing almost boyish. "But never mind – there is always tomorrow . . . and there always will be a tomorrow with its failures and successes, which is as it should be because without the one we could not have the other. You agree?"

She had agreed, but she had lain awake on her bunk bed for a long time, sensing the slight movement of the ship under her and thinking about John Christopher. At one point she had suddenly had the unexpected but strong urge to tell him about her husband — not once had he asked her whether she was married or widowed or what – but in the end she kept silent. Nobody wanted to hear about other people's troubles; most had enough of their own to cope with.

*   *   *   *

Lying in their bunks, both awake, Lily's travelling clock on the long combined dressing table and chest of drawers that ran between their bunks on the seaward side of the cabin showing that it was half past eight, both of them aware that there was a different movement to the ship than they had known before . . . a feeling as though she had come more alive, thought Lily, who had a fanciful streak in her and then, for she was an intelligent young lady, suddenly realizing that by now they must have cleared the English Channel and were beginning to cross the Bay of Biscay. Her father – now long dead but still vividly remembered – had told her as a schoolgirl how he had crossed it in a troop ship bound with his regiment for the Mediterranean and Algiers and had said with pride that while most of his mates were taken with seasickness he had remained as chirpy as a bird – seagull, perhaps – and enjoyed every minute of it, which he hadn't expected because just taking a steamer trip up the Thames to Henley used to put him out of commission. Funny about her father . . . a lovely man, not too clearly remembered except in isolated memories . . . lovely pieces, as it were, of a human jigsaw which she would never be able to put completely together now that her mother was long dead before she had grown to an age of confidences or tender reminiscences. But she knew enough from her aunt to realize that he had been a good husband, a jolly man, and over-generous – give the coat off his back to a beggar, he would, her aunt often said, and the same with everything else. Generous to a fault. But a lovely man . . .

From across the cabin Suzie, head half muffled in her blanket, said, "I think it's got rougher and it's doing different things than it was when we went to bed."

"I expect it is. The last thing you had was coffee and a large glass of Grand Marnier."

"And so did you."

"Yes – but I didn't drink it all. When he wasn't looking I poured half of it into What's-his-name's glass."

"What you mean? What's-his-name? You know his name. It's Richard Linton – Call-me-Dick. And a very nice kind of bloke. But he wants feeding up and some sea air to put the colour back into his cheeks. He bought us both the drinks. Grand Marnier. Never had that before. Glass of port is more my line." She paused, gave a little giggle, and said, "You know it really is true . . . something my father told me. You know he did work, a few years before he was married, as a barman . . . I think it was on the Frank Something Line –"

"Fred Olsen, you mean."

"Maybe, or perhaps that's his brother, but anyway, my father – not married then – ran one of the bars, and did very well for himself until he fell victim, as they say, to his own job. Elbow lifting. But anyway, he didn't miss much. Don't know, if it comes to that – 'cos he said to me in private before we left – and that was difficult – you try finding somewhere private in our house –"

"Suzie!"

"All right. He said, 'Suzie, you watch out, 'cos I've seen it, my girl. People go aboard one thing but once the anchor is weighed and they feel the first lift of the ocean on the deck

80

run under their feet . . . well, then they begin to change. The good Lord rules from above still – but he leaves a lot to old Father Neptune! My old man's a funny one, I can tell you, when he gets going. It's those damned idle brothers of mine I find so trying. So all I'm saying is . . . you just watch out. Some men are like tigers prowling in a jungle . . . and others, bless 'em, are angels from heaven."

Lily laughed and said, "You're a real caution, Suzie. I never heard you talk like this before."

"Maybe not – but it's all been there waiting for the right moment. And now I'm going to get up, have a bath, dress and go down and have a proper breakfast – cornflakes, egg . . . no, eggs and never mind the weight-watching just yet, and bacon and then toast and marmalade. And don't worry – I see where it said that they run weight watchers and keep fit sessions daily, so I shall join up."

She sat up in bed suddenly, a full bodied, handsome young woman, eyes sparkling, the smile of the week on her face and with a little, almost infantile clapping together of her hands, said, "I'm away from it all – and all thanks to you, my dear Lily. I'm going to enjoy everything and after that I'll have memories nobody can take from me – and if I get seasick, then I do. There's always a black joker in the pack somewhere. But who cares?" She paused and then, with a little puckering of her eyebrows, cocked her head at Lily and said almost archly, "You rather fancied him, didn't you?"

Lily said sharply, "Don't be daft."

*   *   *   *

Walking round the promenade deck well before breakfast, John Christopher fell in with Captain Frank Langton, who greeted him with a cordial good-morning and the two – Frank Langton changing direction – fell in together and continued their walk.

Langton said, nodding across the great stretch of open sea, the light of the fast-rising sun gilding the smooth run of the waves, "Best time of the day. Everything fresh . . . and a new day giving us all another chance of perhaps doing better than we did with yesterday. Not that yesterday wasn't by any means pleasant or uneventful. Lovely to smell the air." He raised his head and sniffed as though he were a hound dog.

John Cristopher laughed and said, "Gives you an appetite for breakfast, too. You had this kind of holiday before?"

"No – first time. Like this, that is. But I did some trooping in the Army."

"What were you?"

"Royal Artillery. North Africa, then Sicily and Italy. I was lucky. Never got touched." For a moment he was tempted to embroider the dull truth of his service days miles from the scene of any serious action but, with the first words of a well- known recital of his highly coloured army exploits on the tip of his tongue, he suddenly said (and could hardly believe his own ears): "I was one of the lucky ones . . . always at base. Away from the action."

John Christopher smiled and said, "They also serve who only stand and wait."

"I know. But in some ways . . . well . . ." Langton dropped into silence.

"Well, what? You make me curious, Mr Langton."

"Oh, nothing . . . Well, no. Yes, there is something. Something every man should be aware of."

"Like what?"

"Well, like knowing himself. Finding out about himself. Lots of chaps you'd have thought were as meek and mild as could be . . . real sissies, perhaps. Well . . . when the crunch came they . . . well, they suddenly changed. Their real self came out and they discovered they were full of guts . . . courage . . . the stuff of heroes. I often wondered . . . well, would I have dashed out and rescued some wounded soldier under fire . . ? a pal, say, or even an officer whose guts I hated?"

"You feel strongly about this?"

82

"I suppose so. But –" he grinned – "it doesn't keep me awake at nights."

John Christopher said, "I think it has to be like that for everyone – though few people realize it – that you don't know exactly what you are or are capable of doing in an emergency until the emergency actually turns up."

"I wouldn't quarrel with that." He paused for a moment or two in his talk, the two of them matching step for step along the deck, the great expanse of the wind-swept, sun-gilded sea stretching away to lose itself in the distant curtain of the far sky. Then suddenly he said, "Do you mind if I ask you a personal question?"

"No, of course not. But I might not answer it."

"Well, have I seen you before?"

"Surely that's a question only you can answer."

"I think I have. It was late one night in our local church. I was alone there and I saw you come down from the altar. I was sitting in a pew – they're big box affairs and you might not have seen me."

"Where was this?"

"Redcaster. Quite recently."

"Ah, yes. Of course. I was there on business and I walked down to the church from my hotel. Sometimes late of an evening I like to visit a church and say my prayers. Well . . . fancy that. And what were you doing there, Mr Langton . . . so late?"

"Well, much the same as you, I suppose. Though I'm not quite sure whether it was praying in the way you mean. I just like being there and thinking about myself and wondering."

"Wondering?"

"About one's self. And being different. I mean – although I know I do it – I sometimes talk a bit exaggerated about myself. Particularly about the war years and what I did – when in fact I never was anywhere where there was anything to do that called for . . . well, for courage and action. And, worse still, I was glad it was like that."

83

John Christopher laughed and then said, "You were worried about that?"

"Yes. I would have liked it if . . . well, if I'd been born differently . . . more like most of the other chaps. The ones who really were heroes. I suppose in our hearts that's how we all would like to be . . . I mean people like me . . . you know, rescuing maidens in distress . . . diving into the sea to save someone from drowning –" he laughed suddenly "– or, you know, like in some of the books I used to read as a boy . . . well, being considered a weakling and then one day standing up to the school bully and giving him a good hiding."

John Cristopher laughed and shook his head and then said, "You know what you are? You're a romantic – and that's a dangerous thing to be."

"Why?"

"Because most ordinary people know all about themselves – and are quite comfortable that way. But for others, the romantics . . . well, they're never quite sure what they are or what they will do until the right opportunity or situation is sprung on them. Blessed are the meek, for they shall inherit the earth . . ."

Frank Langton laughed. "I don't want the earth. What would I do with it?"

"It doesn't literally mean the earth. Or inherit. It means, I think, that they shall find something they've always wanted or, perhaps, haven't even guessed they wanted."

Frank Langton laughed and shook his head. "It's too early in the morning for me to take all that in."

"Then let's go and have breakfast."

In the restaurant at their table they found four other people – no longer strangers but people bonded and, indeed, welcoming simply because they were all sharing their meals with one another. The table was the centre of their little community. In time it would widen as they would find that, unlike being ashore, here on the S.S. *Andreas* they were isolated from the world and, through some strange sea alchemy, a great many shore inhibitions and niceties of

84

behaviour were almost unconsciously abandoned. You sat down in a deck chair and someone came and sat beside you and there was complete freedom to talk or not to talk but there was always a smile and a friendly nod, the paperback or the book borrowed from the ship's library lowered for a moment or two and an accord silently made.

At the breakfast table now James Goodbody, one of the rare types who went late to bed and rose early, needing almost half as much sleep as most people, gave them a good-morning but really paid them little attention, for he had chosen a table seat which gave him an oblique profile view of the woman at the next table. More than that, as he had come to his table and sat down she had half turned and the faintest of acknowledgements had passed between them. It had been enough to give the new day a start which, he was sure, would find this slight occasion improved on. No pushing, no brashness . . . no, there was already between them, he romantically liked to think, some seed of mutuality . . . which waited patiently on time. He was not in love yet, nor could she be – but plants of healthy growth break slowly through the top soil . . . no fast, weedy growth. Here, he was convinced – not for the first time in his life – was the promise of the beginning of . . . what? His salvation? True love, finally to be duly and in orthodox fashion blessed, consecrated and consummated. No nonsense; no funny stuff. With this ring I thee wed . . . and he had seen that her left hand was free of any engagement ring. Yes, hope as usual sprang eternal in his breast. He had some money, could exaggerate it a little . . . ho, trifles to be explained and kissed away later. But this time it was love. If it wasn't he would like to know what it was because he had never felt this way before . . . well, not as strongly this way. He saw her now begin to make the motions to rise from the breakfast table – she had a good appetite, which pleased him . . . cornflakes, two fried eggs and a rasher of bacon, toast and marmalade and coffee (women who toyed with food would do the same thing with men).

As he saw the gathering motion of her shoulders rising from the table, he stood up, moved to her chair and adroitly pulled it from her to give her room to turn and leave the table.

For a moment or two they were face to face and then, to his surprise but not dismay, she smiled broadly and said, "Thank you. That was most kind of you." She inclined her head and moved away and he watched her go and distantly there echoed in his mind a snatch – one among many – of not always perfectly recollected gems (as his mother called them) from the *Oxford Book of English Verse* . . .

> *Whenas in silks my Julia goes,*
> *Then, then (me thinks) how sweetly flowes*
> *That liquefaction of her clothes.*

As she disappeared he sighed gently and applied himself with healthy appetite to his plate of eggs and bacon. A widening sense of confidence was beginning to run through him – as it did sometimes at the card table – that things would fall right for him. But almost remote from this conviction was the inner confidence he had that after all these years – which had not been devoid of female companionship and more than a few affairs seriously embarked on only to prove insubstantial more or less quickly – he was on the verge of the 'real thing', so that for the first time the romantic in him was rousing itself with a confidence and vigour never experienced by him before. In some ways there was a faint similarity, but faint indeed, to the feeling he had when he knew that the cards were going to be good to him.

An hour later, carrying a paperback and looking for a sheltered deck spot to spend some time reading, he strolled along the port side of the promenade deck and saw Miss Picton sitting in a deck chair in the glass-enclosed run of part of the bow section of the deck. Quite close to her was an empty deck chair. Whether the conjunction of the deck chairs was fortuitous or not he wasted no time in debating.

Why question what the gods by chance or design sent?

He gave her a smile, just touched the peak of his cloth cap and sat down in the empty deck chair, saying "May I? Or were you keeping it for your mother?"

"No. She's gone to the hairdresser. Anyway – if there's even a little wind going she doesn't care to sit out on the open deck."

"Then . . . if you have no objection?"

"None at all."

"Good. I'm James . . . James Goodbody."

"Picton's my name. Gloria." She made a grimace. "Ghastly, isn't it? But mostly I'm called Ria. I do have a second name, too – but that's not much help to me. My father chose it, or insisted on it because it was a family name. He's dead."

"I'm sorry."

"No need. I hardly remember him. It happened when I was six or seven."

"What is your second name?"

"Erica. The girls at school used to call me Little. 'Erica, or Little by Little.' Ghastly, isn't it?"

"Well . . . I don't know. I think I like it."

"Nice of you to say so."

"On the whole, you know, I think people fuss too much about names. If you think about it: when two people – I mean the opposite sex . . . say in friendship, or are engaged or married, names aren't used so much. It's *darling* or *love* or *angel* or *sweetheart* –" he grinned, and added, "or sometimes *bastard* or *bitch* or . . . well, I'm sure you could add to the list."

"Probably."

"You've cruised before?"

She hunched her shoulders briefly and gave him a wide open grin under raised eyebrows, thinking to herself that somewhere a door was opening . . . no, a window and a warm wind was lazing through, stirring the curtains and bringing with it the warm scents and fragrances of flowers and herbs and the high-placed song of some soaring bird –

87

and she let her shoulders drop because it had all happened before and never gone right, so why should it be any different this time. . . ? Her mother would, when she sensed what was happening, take over and force and spoil things . . . probe and question in a way that sometimes made her wonder why she didn't have a set of forms printed with all the questions clear in print . . . and a big space left under financial resources. Not that it mattered, because she had long ago made up her mind that when Mr Right came along . . . the real Mr Right . . . she wouldn't care if he were dwarf or giant sized, had a big or small head, had two left hands and two right feet . . . well, maybe that was exaggerating, but anyway . . . so long as he had the means to keep her well off the poverty line and she liked him. Liking people, she thought, was so much more important than loving them. Experience had dimly convinced her that there was still an unnamed element which both parties had to have in order to live together for life in harmony and uncursed by some never-to-be-satisfied driving ambition, and unplagued by pretensions to be what they weren't or to be envious of those who had been born with silver spoons in their mouths or a title that went back to William the Conqueror. In even other ways, for all her appearance and demeanour, she was far from being a run of the mill person, she often told herself. Too many people were that way and thought that settling down and looking forward to a dream life as laid out by the advertisements in the society and women's magazines was all there was to have of worth in the world.

Thinking all this, she replied, "Most years. Sometimes twice in the year. Do you?"

"Almost regularly once at least a year. I gamble for a living – or rather to supplement a small private income. Plenty of mugs come aboard and even some who normally know what they're doing let themselves go. Ozone, I think it is." He laughed. "Rash bids and shipboard romances – all due to ozone."

She laughed too and he liked the way she let her head go

back slowly and exposed the long line of her beautiful throat. Then, after reversing the process, in stillness eyeing him for a moment or two, she said, "I like you – but don't waste your time with me. Mamma won't like it and she'll show it."

"Do I have permission to try?"

"Be my guest. Pity you haven't got a title. With that I think she would be prepared to make concessions. After all if I were Lady . . . Lady what?"

He laughed. "Lady Goodbody."

"Ah, yes. Oh, dear, I hadn't thought about that." She gave him a warm grin. "Lady Goodbody – even just Mrs Goodbody. Oh, no."

He shook his head and said, "You're jumping fences you'll never have to come to. You see, I'd change my name by deed poll. Before our marriage. So it's up to you to think of one you'd like."

She laughed then, full-throated, her shoulders shaking, and he laughed with her. Then, suddenly mock serious, he said, "I think I'd call myself Sir Reginald Fullhouse or Sir Barnaby Trumps."

Still laughing she said, "Oh, what a pity. I've always liked the word bezique."

"Then bezique it is. Monsieur le Comte de Bezique. Is it a deal?"

"It's a deal."

"Then the moment I meet your mother I shall formally ask her for your hand in marriage."

Suddenly her face clouded and in a sharp change of voice she said, "Don't you do anything like that. She hasn't got much sense of humour. You see, I had a father who wouldn't have won any prizes in the matrimonial stakes. . . . Oh, Lord – why am I telling you all this?"

He sat down in the empty seat at her side, resisted the desire to take her hand comfortingly, and said, "Don't worry. I won't put my foot in it. And I'm sorry this came up. Trouble is, I rush my fences a bit. I just wanted to meet you and get to know you – so I plunged in."

"You don't have to apologize. I just wanted you to know the form. But I think it would be a good idea for you to go away now. When my mother comes I'll tell her that you stopped and made yourself known and we talked briefly. Then that'll mean when I meet you again and she's with me, I can introduce you and then . . . well . . . things will be . . . well . . ."

"On an even keel?"

"That's right." Then she shook her head with a sharp touch of surprise, "My goodness, how did things get to this stage so quickly?"

He grinned and said, "Because with some people . . . the right people, well, that's the way it is." He touched the peak of his cap in farewell and turned away saying, "I'll see you some time. Keep smiling."

She watched him go and become lost to sight as he turned with the promenade run around the ship's stern. Relaxing into her deck chair she breathed slowly and sleepily as though she had been unduly exerting herself . . . which was what she felt, too, since it was clear to her that she had spoken and acted in a way which was quite foreign to her. Although she was far from gauche or shy there was a large core of reserve in her nature which made her respond to strangers at first with a politeness that hid the natural caution in her where men were concerned. All her mother wanted for her was a good, solidly based marriage in contrast to all that her own had been. And this man James Goodbody, she knew, would be far from being considered suitable by her mother.

*   *   *   *

Richard Linton had come over to where she was sitting alone in the Meridian Room, smiled a little nervously and said, "Do you mind if I join you? Perhaps, too –" his words were hurried almost nervously, "We might have a mid-morning glass of sherry together?"

90

Now as they sat talking over their drinks, Lily thought how very shy he was when it came to women. Not lost for words but shy about looking you full in the face. Not meaning anything shady about him or having something to hide . . . like people were sometimes when they were trying to put one over on you but didn't have much confidence in their success . . . No, he was really shy . . . the kind that thought there was nothing interesting about them and that they didn't have anything much of interest to say. They weren't really like it, of course, because with other men– and she'd seen him about already chatting to other men in the Meridian bar over drinks before lunch – all their reserve vanished. It was just women that changed them . . . like, she giggled inwardly to herself, like they felt at home with a plain, honest no-nonsense cup and saucer from the works canteen, but suddenly all of a tremble and anxiety with a woman – as though they were the most precious of Dresden china. Maybe, though it was something to do with his breakdown. His words echoed fresh in her mind as he now went on talking . . . "I started this small garden centre with not enough help and – I soon found out – not enough money. But I wasn't going to be done. I just got a fixation about it. *I was going to make it go.*"

He paused suddenly, gave her a smile and said, "Is all this boring you?"

"Of course not. But you were daft to try to do so much on your own. No wonder you had a bit of a breakdown."

"Well, it's different now. I've got a partner. He's much older than me. Used to be in the nursery business once. He's retired but can't keep away from it. Doctor said that if I didn't take a break . . . sea air or what have you . . . he wouldn't be responsible." He laughed. "You know how they talk. But anyway – since I hadn't had a break for three years I thought I would. And I must say even the short time I've been aboard I begin to feel different. You interested in plants, Miss Franklin?"

91

"Yes, I am. But not your way – though, of course, I like all flowers and so on. What's your favourite?"

"Oh, I don't know . . . Well, yes, I do. I think lilac. When I was a boy we lived in a house where there was a great hedge of it all up the driveway to the front of the house. But what do you mean, not in my way?"

"Well, you're an expert . . . you know . . . on growing things . . . a horti . . ."

"Horticulturist?"

"Yes. Just growing things. But all flowers have special meanings, too. So that's why I asked what your favourite is. Purple or white lilac?"

He grinned. "Well, I like both."

For a moment or two she was silent. His cheerful grin had touched her in some odd way, it deeply grooved his cheeks and gave him a merry puckish look like . . . Oh, dear . . . who? And then she remembered . . . her father . . . raising his eyebrows and listening gravely to some long-winded tale she was telling of what she had done all day while he had been away.

"No – you've got to choose."

"Must I?"

"Yes."

"All right. Let's see . . . Well, I think white."

"White . . . Now then, let me think. Ah, yes. That means youthful innocence." She grinned. "Are you young and innocent?"

"I refuse to answer that question. What do I get with the purple?"

For a moment or two Lily was silent, and then said "You really want to know?"

"Of course."

"I don't think I can."

"Oh, come on."

"No, I can't."

"That's not fair . . . not even if it's because you know I'm going to fall overboard. I could always go around with a life jacket on. Come on – play fair." He gave her a teasing grin and reached out and took her right hand. "Come on – for better or for worse. Let me have it."

"All right." She turned her head from him avoiding his eyes, and said, "It means – first ever emotions of love."

For a moment or two there was a silence between them as they looked at one another and, while her own lips trembled a little to match the emotional tremble of her body, he reached out and took her right hand and said "Well, then that's O.K., isn't it?"

*　　*　　*　　*

Lying in bed early the next morning, Suzie woke, yawned and stretched her arms and then relaxed and knew at once that something was wrong. Sleepily she called across to Lily, "What's the matter, Lil? We don't seem to be moving."

"Of course we don't. We are at Gibraltar. We docked about an hour ago and after breakfast we're going ashore so that we can see all the sights and drive up to the top of the Rock and see the monkeys or apes or whatever they call them. This is a very famous place in British history."

"So what? I never did like history much. Nor geography. But I was good at sums. You know some shops try to short-change you – but they don't do it to me. I met a girl who told me – she worked in a big baker's and confectioner's shop what had a little tea saloon as well – that it would surprise you how very few people ever check their change. Just take it and pocket it . . . and plenty more where that came from. But not me. Not even if I married the Aga Khan."

"He's married already."

"Makes no difference. He can have as many wives as he likes." She yawned. "So what do we do today?"

"You know perfectly well. We're going to get a car and motor all up and around the Rock . . . see the monkeys or whatever they are and whatever else is going."

"Apes they are. Barbary apes."

93

"Well, what's the difference?"

"Anyway . . . nasty smelly things – you don't catch me going near them."

"You can always stay in the car."

"I shall because I got no head for heights. I go all weak at the knees and giddy."

"I wonder you're bothering to come."

"Well, I don't want to miss anything, do I? First thing my lot will ask me is whether I saw all the monkeys on the Rock."

"Apes."

"Same thing as far as I'm concerned."

"Well, whatever it is – if we don't get some breakfast soon all the taxis will have gone and we'll have to stay aboard."

An hour later they had breakfasted in their cabin and joined the waiting crowd at the head of the shore-going gangway down to the quayside where a long queue of waiting hire cars werc lined up to take the ship's sightseers. There was no standing on ceremony or little parties keeping together. The passengers just crowded into the taxis as they came along so that families and friends sometimes became separated.

As the two girls came off the gangway and hurried towards the slow-moving line of waiting taxis they were joined by John Christopher, who took them each by the arm, gave them a merry grin and said, "I didn't see you at breakfast this morning?"

"No," said Suzie. "We were very posh and had it in our cabin – in bed, or bunk should I say? I haven't had breakfast in bed since my mother died." She laughed, "I couldn't see my father or any of my brothers bringing me up a breakfast tray. Mind you though I really do prefer a sit-up affair at a proper table."

John Christopher said, "You must .tell me about your family sometime. They seem an interesting lot to me."

"Well, don't start her off now," said Lily. "Or when I'm

94

around. Just the thought of them gives me the willies. I know what I'd do –"

Her words were cut short by the arrival of one of the long queue of cars to take them off on their excursion. The two girls got into the back seat while John Christopher sat on a little pull down jump seat facing them.

Suzie said, "Why don't you sit up front with the driver? You'd be more comfortable."

"Because I like to be in here with you two charmers. Anyway the driver won't move off until he's full up so you could have had a stranger –"

Lily interrupted him with a laugh and said, "No stranger we've got Captain Langton." She nodded frontwards to where Langton was taking the spare seat on the driver's bench. As he settled he looked back at them, and grinned, saying, "Morning all. Lucky man. Last seat. Charming company. Mrs Bell's not coming ashore. She's got no head for heights and she doesn't like monkeys, she says."

"Apes," said John Christopher as they moved off.

"I know," said Langton. "Every Army man knows about 'em. If they ever die out, the saying goes, then that will be the end of British occupation of the Rock." He thumped the end of his heavy walkingstick on the floor and added, "Tradition and Superstition. All countries have them . . . swear by them, right or wrong. Belief is the thing. You got belief. You got faith . . . well then you've got a head start over the rest of the chaps what don't have 'em."

John Christopher smiled teasingly and said, "Of course – but one must be modest about it, mustn't one?"

"That too," Captain Langton agreed. "No boasting. Show me the biggest boaster in a group of men and you'll also be more than likely looking at the biggest all-talk-and no doer. You agree, Mr Christopher?"

"You put it very well. Yes, I agree."

At this moment the car moved off and their tour had begun of what was once known to the Greeks and the Romans as one of the renowned Pillars of Hercules . . . sail far enough beyond them and – in the old days people believed you would topple off the edge of the world – or so said John Christopher, who was giving the commentary with a cheeky grin on his face. Its upper slopes, he told them ("I've read it all up in a book before I came on the cruise," he was honest enough to confess to them) in Spring were thick with wild narcissus and colonized with wild apes originally brought over by the early Moorish settlers as pets. And tradition had it that if the apes died out then British possession of the Rock would cease – so when they began to decrease during World War Two, Sir Winston Churchill gave instructions that new blood was to be obtained from Morocco and more apes were brought over. . . . All this he told them as the driver made his way through the town and up the long, twisting climb to the heights of the Rock. When for a moment he paused for breath Captain Langton broke in with slightly ponderous sincerity, pleased to have a captive audience, and said, "Tradition and Superstition are all very well, but plain facts rule all matters. I never served here but I know a lot of chaps who did. Some marvellous engineering works went on here. The Rock is three miles long and one thousand four hundred feet high and there's no water up here at all except what they get from what is called catchment areas . . . big, smooth sloping concrete areas on the hillside from which they channel off the rainfall . . . marvellous engineering . . . and then they run it –"

Breaking in upon him Lily said, "I don't think I'd like to live anywhere up here . . . like the soldiers in their barracks. I've got no head for heights."

"Nor me," said Suzie.

"Well . . ." said Captain Langton, "some have and some haven't. It's not something that's ever bothered me."

Some time later, after the long twisting climb, the car drew up on a small piece of parking ground close to a small café and the entrance to St Michael's Cave – a limestone cavern, so the driver informed them, famous for its stalactites and stalagmites and which was often used for ballet and concerts.

The floodlighting too had to be seen for it brought out all the natural beauty of the cave. However both Suzie and Lily wanted first to feed the apes . . . the car driver obliging, having with him some packets of peanuts which he sold to them.

They all joined the small knot of sightseers already at the guard rail at the top of the steep long fall down the rock side, a fall covered here and there with low scrub growth . . . while, hundreds of feet below, the sea spread out in a great dazzling vastness of sun sparkle and foam-tipped waves raised by a strong southerly wind. And here just beyond the guard rail – some even coming over the rail for the food offered by the sightseers – were the apes, young and old and all long used to the attention of the tourists and appreciative of the nuts, fruit and sweets offered to them. Some of the adults had small spring-born young clinging to them. And it was here that trouble struck.

As Lily and Suzie leaned on the guard rail watching the antics of the younger apes among the rocks of the steep fall of the sloping hillside, one of them came ambling up to the rail and held out a paw to a woman standing next to Suzie, begging for peanuts. But the woman shook her head and turned away . . . all her peanuts gone. At this the ape turned away, sidled along the slope below the rail to Lily and Suzie and held out his arms, hands cupped to them for some contribution. However, neither of them had any peanuts left either.

Suzie said, "There's a chap selling bags of nuts over there, I'll go and –"

She was turning away as she spoke when the young ape, having now climbed to the topmost rail of the guard fence reached out a paw and pulled free from under Suzie's right arm the handbag she was carrying slung over her shoulder. Before she could hold on to it, the ape had snatched it away and ambled some way down the steep slope with it where, after turning it over curiously a few times, he dropped it and went lolloping on all fours to join a group of young apes that

97

were scampering after one another in play further along the slope.

Her voice high with alarm, Suzie cried, "My handbag! My bag . . . Oh, the thieving rascal . . ! Oh, heavens . . . my passport and all my money! Oh, what shall I do?"

Captain Langton took her by the arm and said soothingly, "Don't worry. There must be a keeper around. We'll –"

"That's no good," wailed Suzie. "They'll start playing with it and – well, can't somebody go down and get it? It's only a little way down. Couldn't you do that, Captain Langton?"

Langton looked down the slope. Fortunately at this moment the apes were showing no interest in the bag. Further along the guard rail two parties were distributing largesse and attracting all their attention.

Frank Langton said, "It's better to get the keeper."

"But it might be too late. Oh, my passport and . . . Oh, Lordie some of my traveller's cheques, too," she wailed, putting her hands to her cheeks and shaking her head so that Lily slipped an arm around her and made soothing noises.

Meantime Frank Langton stood at the rail, holding it in both hands and staring at the bag only a few yards down the slope, and then at the onward fall of the slope . . . down, down . . . far, far below lay the sea and . . . he choked and swallowed hard on his fear and raged inwardly at himself . . . climb the rail, nothing, go down the slope, nothing . . . a bit slippery, loose earth and rock litter . . . be a man . . .

His eyes moved again to the long, long fall and he had to shut his eyes and breathe hard . . . he was a soldier, a man of action, and . . . Oh God – why couldn't he just go straight ahead and do it? Why? Why?

He looked around, saw the worried faces of Suzie and Lily and then John Christopher watching him as though – all this flashing through his tormented mind in a few seconds – he waited to see what he would do . . . as though he had made some bet with himself . . . no, as though . . . Oh God!

98

"They'll get it and tear everything to pieces," wailed Suzie, and she stamped a foot with impatience.

Then to his relief – and his excuse forming for afterwards *... Gammy leg you know ... Cassino ... pieces of shrapnel still in it ... some days plays me up worse than ever ... today's one of 'em ... don't show it, but it's there* – he watched as John Christopher put a hand on the top rail and a foot on the lower and began to lever himself up, but at this moment a voice said, "O.K. Johnny – leave it me. If the apes make any trouble I can speak their language."

And there, come from the touring car which had followed them, was James Goodbody, flanked by Mrs and Miss Picton, and in no time at all Goodbody was over the rail and sliding down the loose slope, and had recovered the handbag. A couple of the apes sidled curiously towards him as he climbed back but he shooed them off with a wave of his arm and finally climbed over the rail and with a mock, but smiling bow, handed her bag to Suzie who was so overcome that she put her arms around him and gave him a kiss which – since a little crowd had gathered beyond the rail, wondering what was going on – raised a brief cheer to which James Goodbody responded with the merest sketch of a bow.

Watching all this were Mrs and Miss Picton and, as Goodbody walked across to join them after his deed of daring, Mrs Picton said to her daughter, "Well – I will say he's got spirit and courage and a good presence – but gambling, my dear, for a living ... really, do you think so?"

"No, I don't. And I don't think he does, really. Though I'm not sure."

"And you'd take a chance?"

Gloria smiled. "Doesn't everybody when they get married?"

"Maybe ... maybe – but I beg of you not to rush things. I'm an indulgent mother, but I've no high opinion of men. They either go to pieces too easily or they are granite hard."

"None of them ever comfortable?"

"My dear child – don't ever marry a comfortable man. It's

99

like trying to cross a moorland bog in the dark. You never know where the next step is going to land you. *Goodbody* – I don't like that. Perhaps you could arrange to pronounce it – Goad-bow-dee?"

"I think, dear Mamma," said Gloria, "that you are thinking much too far ahead. Just because –"

"Fatal words, my dear," said her mother. "And favourites of your dear, improvident father . . . 'I didn't mean to. It was just because when I dropped into the club there was old who-ever-it-was back from America,' and so on and so on . . . And all this at three o'clock in the morning and more often than not his wallet empty and more too dispensed in IOUs or repayment sworn the following day on the word of a gentleman. Gentleman, I'll say he was, but where money was concerned . . . well, well, I don't have to tell you. Thank God, unknown to him I regularly raided his wallet and managed to put something aside for us."

"But he must have known you were doing it, Mamma?"

"Of course he did. But he was too much of a gentleman ever to say or show that he knew. I'll give him that. He was a gentleman from top to toe – but I'll tell you there were often times when I found that no compensation at all . . . no comfort at all for having picked the wrong man. And when I think –"

"I know, mother. But we must go. They're all waiting for us in our car."

*　　*　　*　　*

Later in the afternoon of that day the S.S. *Andreas* pulled away from her berth alongside the South Mole in the Royal Navy Dockyard and headed out of harbour on the long run across the Mediterranean to the Greek islands.

That evening as a cloudless darkness hung like a great canopy over the sea Captain Frank Langton sat in a deck chair alongside Mrs Nancy Bell on the sheltered port side of the promenade deck after having made three turns round the

deck to settle their dinner and to enjoy the increasing
warmth of the evening air.

"South wind, Nancy, my dear. Blowing straight from
Africa." He sniffed once or twice vigorously to savour it.

Mrs Bell said, "You haven't got a cold, have you Frank?"

"No, of course not, my dear. Just taking the smell of Africa
. . . brings back old memories. Remember once . . . just
before Tunis fell, it was –"

"Frank."

There was if still friendly a note of authority in her voice
. . . even command, he thought for a fleeting and surprised
moment or two.

"What's the matter, my love?"

"Nothing. Not with me. It's you, my dear. Why do you do
it? I like you very much. I could even say . . . love you very
much. But you worry me, my dear. You see, I think you're
asking for something you don't need."

"What do you mean, my dear?"

"Well, you mustn't be cross with me if I say it – I only do it
because I love you. And I love you just as you are – not what
you think you ought to be."

"And I love you. And I want you to be proud of –"

"That's where the trouble is. You think you have to prove
or do something to show people that you really are the brave
captain . . . the fearless soldier. Fearless, Why, there's no
such thing for anybody. You don't get rid of fear – you just
keep it in its place, covered up."

"But Nancy, what –"

"No, let me finish. I was with the party behind you today,
though you didn't see me. Our car arrived after yours. And I
saw that ape thing take Suzie's handbag. You see I changed
my mind at the last minute and decided to join you all on the
Rock. Listen, dear – I don't think anyone else would have
known – but I know you too well. You could have gone down
for the handbag well before Mr Goodbody."

"But I didn't. Oh, God, Nancy – only because heights
really put me off."

"So they do hundreds of people. There's nothing to be ashamed of." She reached out a hand and took his and went on, "You don't have to show people you're a hero or that you're a battle-tired soldier. Oh . . . Frankie – just be content with being yourself. You're a very nice man. Now, I'm going to say one thing more and then I'm going to leave you to think about it. I wouldn't say this if you weren't very special to me. I just want you to go on being the way God made you . . . a nice, pleasant, honest man who would knowingly never do harm to anybody . . . a nice caring man whom I love very much and who loves me. You don't have to make up stories of your past. Just tell it straight . . . what you were and what you've done." She laughed gently. "Oh, don't look so glum, Frankie, you won't be alone. The world is full of Frank Langtons. But remember, because I know this about you, if you'd been all alone up there today and someone like a small boy or girl had fallen over and were in danger or whatever . . . well, you would have been after them like a shot . . . without a thought for yourself."

Weakly he said, "I wish I could think that. Oh, Nancy . . . I can't help it – it's something inside me. As though I've got to make up for something. All those fancy war stories . . . Oh, Lord. What must you think of me?"

She laughed, surprising him, the sound light and pleasing on the night air and said, "I'll tell you. I like you and I love you. And I respect your longing to have been a hero. So, love . . . Oh, Frankie, I had to say it . . . I've longed to for months. But now it's done and only because . . . well, because I love you and I know you love me but if –"

He reached out suddenly and took her near hand and bent over and kissed it briefly and then said, "Oh, Nance . . . Oh, what can I say? You know the truth about me. What can I do or say?"

She stood up then, came closer and bent and kissed him on the forehead. Straightening up, she said. "Just be yourself. Be my Frank – the man I love. Now, you just sit there and smoke a last pipe. I'll see you in the morning and tomorrow will be a new day."

With a sudden vigour he said, "By heavens it will. It will. I promise you that, Nancy." He stood up, caught her by the shoulders and kissed her and then released her, seeing for a moment as she turned away the shine of tears in her eyes. He watched her go, knowing she wanted to be alone and then, left to himself, he sat down and began to fill himself a pipe.

A few minutes after he had got it going properly, John Christopher came strolling down the deck wearing a silk shirt, striped with a riot of peacock colours, red drill trousers with a narrow white cording down the sides, bare feet in open-work blue sandals and, perched on his head, a white beret. There would have been a recent time when Frank Langton would have disapproved of his outfit but he realized by now that there was some spirit engendered on a cruise ship which found unexpected flowering in most people. With some it was their manner . . . the shy became gregarious, the reticent became extroverts – or almost so – and apart from formal occasions just as their spirit, their natures flowered exotically, so did their appearance. People, young and old, wore what they fancied, not what they thought others would expect them to wear. Seeing John Christopher approaching, Frank Langton was mildly put out by his costume. Without so much as a *by-your-leave* John Christopher sat down in the vacant seat next to him and said, surprisingly, "You're a conventional man, aren't you? If you see someone dressed up . . . *en fantaisie*, do the French call it? . . . you find yourself mildly disapproving? All right at a fancy dress ball – but not for everyday use. I can't think why not. Cheer the City of London and New York up, wouldn't it?" He laughed and then, leaning back in his chair and putting his clasped hands behind his head, he stared out at the dusk-smoked waste of sea, a few early stars low and bright on the horizon in the west, and said, "I don't want you to take offence at this because I'm absolutely sincere and truthful – not that I can explain why, any more than you can explain why sometimes you know that someone is lying to you or talking in a friendly way when all the time they hate or despise you . . . Waves? Mental . . . psychic . . . mind-reading . . . or just a gift never to be explained in human terms? There are more things in heaven and earth, Horatio – than are dreamt of in your philosophy –"

"Our philosophy," said Captain Langton. "That was the original reading. I remember my English teacher telling me that more years ago than I care to recall."

"So be it. But the point is that I have dreams . . . sometimes dreams in which I get messages for people." He stopped talking and eyed Langton questioningly.

Frank Langton said, "Go on. Why have you stopped?"

"I wasn't sure whether you wanted me to go on."

"Neither am I." Langton suddenly smiled. "But if you want to, I'm very comfortable here. And, good or bad, I'd like to know what you have to say – though I don't promise to believe it. I've had my fortune told a few times in my life and I can't –" he laughed – "remember hearing anything that came true. So you can give me your message without worry."

"Well, ten minutes ago I was in the Dolphin Room having a *crème de menthe* with my cup of coffee – do you like *crème de menthe*?"

"No."

"Funny. Not many men do. I love it. Anyway there I was – and you must believe this – just raising the glass to my mouth to sip when there was a voice inside my head, clear as a bell – quite remarkable . . . I even looked round to see if anyone else could have heard, but they obviously had not –"

"Obviously, since it was inside your head." Frank Langton grinned. This John Christopher was a queer bird, but entertaining and, he was sure, had no vice in him – unless you could call too active an imagination a vice. But, of course, you couldn't. All great men had to have it . . . painters, poets, writers, generals . . .

"Of course – but I must have looked very odd sitting there by myself with a glass of *crème de menthe* stuck half way to my mouth in my raised hand and a glazed look in my eyes as this voice said quite distinctly to me: 'John Christopher, my faithful one, go at once to the Captain Langton and tell him two things. First: that there can be no true shame in being born as you are. For the good you must be grateful and never arrogant; and for the bad or the shaming you must also have a welcome because it means that the good Lord above has marked you out to be tried and in the true moment or moments of challenge to find yourself far from wanting. Just as some seeds lie dormant over years, waiting for the rare season of long-hoped-for rains to make the desert bloom . . . well, so with every man there comes a season of true flowering . . . just once it comes and then, unless a man is wise enough to go a-harvesting then the following years of his near starvation will slowly diminish him. You would be a hero, a man of courage and resource, but you think you know that this can never be because we are all as God has ordained us to be. How wrong! He has done no such thing. Man was created with free will – no matter his inheritance of paternal and maternal genes and characteristics . . .' "

He broke off as Frank Langton stirred comfortably and then very slowly raised himself from his chair and stood looking down at John Christopher in silence, his lips pursed, his face stern as though he marshalled some angry response and paused now to gain the other's full attention before he spoke. Then he suddenly laughed gently and said, "Don't try to tell me anything about myself. It's a subject I've studied in detail all my years. The leopard can't change its spots. Neither can a man alter what he is . . . how he has been born and lumbered for good or for bad with a personality over which he has never had any choice. I know you mean kindly, and I thank you for it. But there is nothing to be done. Not a thing."

Then to John Christopher's surprise he gave a long chuckle and with a broad smile on his face looked at him and, shaking his head, said, "You're an odd bird, you know. Now it's my turn to talk frankly to and about you. There's something . . . well, without offence, I suppose some people would call a bit pushy, a bit enjoying being something of a character. No harm in it, I suppose. Also . . . well, I can't think why I think it but I think that there's more to you than meets the eye."

"Like what?"

"Well . . . like you could be playing a part . . . for some reason, probably a good one . . . well, I hope so. Or, maybe, you're just doing it for your own pleasure . . . acting up. Perhaps you've left the real John Christopher ashore and become a different person. It happens on cruises, you know. When people talk about themselves it's never penny plain . . . always tuppence coloured. I do it myself – Captain Langton, R.A. – Royal Artillery. But really it was R.A.S.C. Royal Army Service Corps – grocers and suppliers to the chaps who put their lives on the line. Not that we don't have to have all that back up. But every man sees himself as a hero – except perhaps the ones who had no choice except to be heroes . . . face to face with the foe." He was silent for a moment and then gave a short laugh. "I've got to say, Mr Christopher, that you're a bit of a card. But at least talking to you is stimulating."

"That's a nice thing to say, Captain Langton. Of course, I know that you think I'm a kind of a crank . . . a pleasant one, I hope. But I did have this voice speak to me about you. In the moment of extreme challenge you will discover your true self."

He stood up, then moved a little towards the rail and, staring out over the starlit sea, spread his arms and said, "How right God was, for even in His great creation he found a place for Man knowing that of all the animals Man would be the least ready to keep his ordained place or the peace with his own kind – but that in the end he would learn and then truly would the great work of the Creation be finished."

"Amen," said Frank Langton and he lay back in his chair and watched John Christopher walk away down the deck, past other passengers sitting out in the balmy night after dinner and the evening concert.

106

SIX

THEY WERE SITTING together at a small coffee table at the far end of the long lounge which was an annexe to the small ship's library. At this end of the lounge was a small bar and a run of banquette seats under the wide windows that gave an extensive view of part of the forward run of the ship and a wide sweep of the sea, creamed-tipped now with a ragged run of breakers under the rude sweep of an easterly force four wind.

Lily watched him as he turned away from the bar, carrying a small tray on which were his own drink and hers and Suzie's. He made his way slowly, not because of the ship's small motion but because he did not want to spill any of the generously filled glasses of medium dry sherry for two and a dry sherry for himself.

"He'd never make a waiter," said Suzie with a slight giggle.

"Why not?" asked Lily.

"Because he keeps looking at the tray to make sure he doesn't spill any. I worked in a pub for four months, the time all my lot were out and on the dole together. You just take the tray, look straight ahead and everything takes care of itself."

Richard Linton came to the table and setting the tray down carefully, said, "Sorry – I've spilled one. I'll have it because –"

"Nonsense," said Lily, taking the glass from which sherry had been spilled.

"But –"

"Don't argue with her," said Suzie. "She's got a terrible temper if she's crossed."

He sat down and grinned at her, and she thought he really was a pleasant looking chap, well mannered too and owning his own nurseries somewhere in Devonshire . . . near Tavistock, wherever that was. Somewhere in the West Country.

He lifted his glass to them and said, "Here's to a life on the rolling waves. Gosh — I've lost count of the days but I feel a different man already."

Lily said, "I think we all feel different because everything is different from the way we normally live."

Suzie laughed. "Different! You can say that again. Being here is like coming out of prison and straight to the Ritz. If I were at home now I'd just have finished clearing the breakfast things away and kicked my lot out of the house from under my feet and starting upstairs to do the bedrooms . . . make the beds and tidy up."

Linton asked, "Don't your brothers and father do things like that?"

"You must be joking."

"But what about now that you're away?"

"No trouble. They get out of the bed in the morning and get back into it at night just as though it were a nest. When it gets too horrible even for them, they get Ma Rudwell to come in from over the road and sort them out. I was away for a month once — visiting a sick aunt in Scotland who my mother had once told me I might have expectations from . . . she being a spinster and — well, when it comes to the pinch you got to leave what little you have and if you don't want to spite nobody it goes to your nearest if not dearest. It didn't, though. She left it all to the Salvation Army."

Linton said, "She could have done worse."

"I know — she could have left it to them and most of it would have gone on drink and the horses. My family are deg . . . degen . . . oh, what is the word?"

Lily smiled and said, "Degenerates? No, I don't think so.

108

They just want jobs . . . being unemployed must be awful. Wanting to do something and then not being able to. Hanging around kicking your heels all day. Some men can take it . . . some fight back — like going out and starting something up for themselves."

Suzie looked at Linton and asked, "Is that what you did?"

He was silent for a while before answering and then with a shrug of his shoulders he said, "Well . . . it wasn't quite like that. You see, I went to a horticultural college first, then I worked for a couple of years at a nursery garden in Kent . . . and, well, eventually I started out on my own. But I was lucky because my father helped by putting up half the capital and I borrowed the other half from the bank by getting a loan with the nursery as security. I cleared that off a year ago. It was hard work though."

"Well, good for you. But you had to pay for it, didn't you?" said Suzie.

"Well . . ."

"Oh, yes you did. That's why you're here. You worked too hard and got all run down and —"

"Suzie," Lily broke in sharply. "That's none of our business. Really . . ."

"Well, she's right. I did overdo it." As he spoke, his glass now empty, he rose from the table, and went on, "Now, if you'll excuse me. I must do my daily exercise. Six times round the promenade deck . . . morning and afternoon . . . great lungfuls of sea air but —" he smiled at Suzie and added "How did you know I'd been ill?"

Suzie laughed. "I'm a great nosey parker. I was sitting next to John Christopher in the big lounge place on the Games Deck where they have the discotheque and you walked by and I said — this'll make you blush — what a nice chap you were and he said that you certainly were and also a gentleman and from a very distinguished family and that your father was a Member of Parliament."

"Yes." He grinned. "But don't broadcast it."

"Of course not," said Lily firmly, "It's nobody else's

109

business but yours. So far as we're concerned you're just a nice bloke who wants lots of rest and peace and quiet to build up after a long and nasty illness."

"That's right. And thank you. Now I must take my morning exercise round the deck . . . six times. I did work it out how far that was but I've already forgotten." He gave them a big smile and moved away.

Watching him go Suzie said, "You know, I think he's got a bit of a thing for you."

"Don't be silly. What would he want with the likes of me?"

"You want me to be coarse?"

"That's enough of that."

"Perhaps there isn't enough of that. That's the trouble. You know my mother come down in the world when she married my father – God knows why she did it, except for love, and there's no rhyme nor reason to that. But they were happy. Our house was a different place when she was alive. We all worshipped her – think of that. Those oafs my brothers and that lazy sod my father – she only had to lift her little pinkie finger and they came a tumbling over one another to see what she wanted done. And so did I. 'Magnetoism', she had."

"Magnetism."

"Yes, that as well. But the thing is she did six years as a lady's maid in a big house over Oxford way. She picked things up quick and could talk and act just like a lady herself – so why did she have to marry an aboriginal like my father – who worked on the production line at Morris Motors, Cowley and was always being laid off four or five months in every year? Not that he ain't got a good heart and all. So you don't have a thing to worry about. Less so these days. I reckon he fancies you. Mrs Richard Linton. . . !"

At this point Suzie burst into a choking spasm of almost unbridled laughter, and Lily – who had known these kind of outbursts before – stood up and with great dignity walked away from her to go to the writing room where she would drop a line to her Aunt Rachel. There were times, she told herself, when Suzie just went too far. Well, she didn't want to be too harsh – perhaps that father and her brothers had something to do with it. It was inevitable that something of their coarseness should rub off on her. Such a pity . . . she was so nice really, and the only true friend she had. And as for Richard Linton . . . rubbish. Someone had told her about shipboard friendships and romances. A week after disembarking one began to forget . . . one had the happiness and joy of the cruise, the meetings and the moments of tenderness . . . warm nights under star-brilliant skies . . . no buses to catch, no washing-up . . . a dream world with only dream people in it . . . yes, that was it . . . one became part of a lovely dream.

At this moment, so deeply immersed in her thoughts was she that Lily bumped into someone coming out of the ship's shop. As she partly stumbled a hand took her arm and held her steady and a familiar voice said, "That's why they have a rail all the way around the main deck."

She looked up to see John Christopher smiling at her, one hand still lightly on her arm, and she said, "I'm sorry – what did you say?"

"That that's why they have a rail all around the deck, to stop people daydreaming and walking straight over the side."

"No fear of that. Though I was in a bit of a huff about something that silly goose of a Suzie said to me."

"Well, I don't suppose she meant to upset you. After all –"
He broke off and then, smiling, took her firmly by the arm and said, "Come on – I'll walk you round the deck and – if you give me something from your handbag . . . anything, a silver pencil, eye-black stick, or a compact . . . anything so that I can just hold it . . . I'll tell you something about your future and –"

"Oh, I don't want any of that kind of nonsense, thank you very much."

"It's not nonsense. You know perfectly well that daffodils will bloom in spring and that the swallows leave England in

III

the late autumn. Everything that lives has a predestined life, an inescapable destiny. You may not believe this but it is true. Some people, not many, can see ahead to what is going to happen in the future to people. Some tell others about this and are either believed or written off as cranks. But these days fewer and fewer people have the gift and now not many of these are prepared to tell other people about it."

"Well . . . I don't know."

He laughed gently and urged, "Come on. So, all right, you don't want to believe what I'll say. Just tell yourself it's all a made-up thing by me. We don't need any special preparations or place to do it."

"Can't we do it just walking round the deck?"

"If you like."

"Would my compact do?"

"Yes . . . anything that is personally yours." He grinned, adding. "Don't look so scared. There was a time thousands of years ago when people had this gift. But then in his wisdom I think the Great Creator had second thoughts and stopped being so liberal with his gifts and –"

"Sometimes, you know," Lily interrupted him, "I don't think you're ever really serious. It's all a front. I think you fancy the whole world and all the people in it are some big joke on the part of . . . well, the part of . . . Oh, I don't know. Here –" she handed him her compact, saying "– do we have to sit down somewhere?"

"Not if you don't want to. Walking's fine. But just don't say anything to me for a few minutes. All right?"

Suddenly Lily laughed. "Why not? But make it as nice as you can."

"We'll see. Now just a few moments' silence."

They walked on slowly together for the whole length of the port side of the promenade deck, past the Wayfarers Tavern, the writing room and then the library, past the photo shop, the reading room and the fruit machine room and then as they rounded the stern John Christopher turned his head and gave her a wide grin, saying,

112

"You've been very good and quiet and you came through beautifully. Quietness from the subject is so important where the future is concerned. The past is not so fuzzy – after all it can't be changed so it has no worries, but the future is touchy. It doesn't like its rhythm disturbed, because then things happen that shouldn't happen and take a long time putting right. But you were a good subject."

"Frankly," said Lily politely but firmly, "I just think you're putting the whole thing on. But anyway . . . if it amuses you it doesn't worry me. Tell me all – the bad and the good. I'm not worried . . . you see I've got –"

"Yes, I know. He's always there to receive our thanks or to listen to our troubles and give us the strength to overcome them. Now – no more of that sermon. Here's what I saw. Just a few pictures."

"No dialogue?"

He laughed. "I like that. A sense of humour is something that my father prizes in people very much and so do I. Away with long faces and –"

"And," interrupted Lily, "you get on and tell me what you saw."

"Well, it wasn't very much – or all that clear."

"Leave the excuses until afterwards."

"All right . . . but they were only just brief pictures. Well, first of all I saw you sitting on a seat . . . a sort of bus-stop seat on a pavement of a long road and you were looking up at something in the sky . . . I couldn't see what and then a man came along. I only had a back view of him. He seemed young and he was carrying an icecream wafer in each hand, one of which he gave to you as he sat down beside you. Then as you faced one another, icecreams in hand, he said something to you and as though totally surprised you gave a little jump and the icecream fell from your hand on to the dusty pavement. And there it lay while you just looked at the young man, who had his back to me, and then you suddenly drooped your head a little and covered your face with the spread of both your hands and I saw, for the first time, that

113

you were carrying a single flower in it . . . a long-stemmed red carnation –"

"A what?"

"A long-stemmed red carnation."

"Oh, dear . . ." Then, with a sharp look at John Christopher, she said, "You're teasing me. Making things up – and don't tell me that you don't know the language of flowers, either."

"No, I don't. Why?"

She laughed then, shaking her head, and said, "Because it's all too pat like. A good line to turn a girl's head. Though I'm sure you haven't got eyes for me. In fact . . . ah, well, never mind. But to satisfy your curiosity, I'll tell you that a red carnation stands for – *Alas, for my poor heart.*"

"Well, I like that. Anyway, now you've been warned. If anyone comes courting you with a red carnation . . . well . . ."

"Well, what – Mister Know All Christopher?"

He smiled. "Well, when that happens you'll have no trouble in knowing what to say or do."

"Doesn't sound very romantic to me – icecream wafers, bus stops and red carnations!"

"Don't take it too literally, it may not be like that at all, it's what you interpret or read into the picture that matters – like for instance the red carnation."

"Well, Mister Christopher – so you say. But don't think you fool me. There's a lot about you that you keep to yourself. And I'm not going to ask you any questions. But sometimes . . . well, it's a bit like that bit in Peter Pan, isn't it? When everyone gets asked whether they believe in fairies. And the word at the heart of the matter is – belief. Am I right?"

"How could I deny it?" He reached out, took her right hand and brushed it with his lips in a courtly and gentle salute before walking away, only, after a few paces, to turn his head over his right shoulder and wink at her so that she laughed out loud, seized with a rare exhilaration and excitement as though she had been given some gift-wrapped present and faced it, trembling on the brink of opening it, knowing that it held the one thing in all the world which she desired. So strong was her emotion that she slowly relapsed into her chair, eyes shut, and began to take long breaths of the sea air as though she had been too long starved of ozone while her imagination rioted through a confliction of fancies too numerous to follow so that she was glad when a voice above her said, "Do you feel in a quick-witted mood this morning?"

She opened her eyes and looked up – as she knew she would because she had recognized his voice – at Richard Linton. He gave her a grin and went on, "There's a bingo session just going to start in the Dolphin Room. I thought perhaps we could form a partnership. Yes?"

"Why, yes, of course, if you want me to. But I'm not very good at it."

"Neither am I – but you never know. Beginner's luck, and all that."

He took her arm as she began to rise and helped her to her feet and then still holding her arm walked with her along the promenade deck forward to the entrance to the Dolphin Room, and as they went – which she knew was nonsense really – the sea seemed lovelier than it had ever been, the long curl of an occasional breaking roller a cascading glory which – banal or not the words came to her – was like some great hoard of pearls being spilled over the carpet of the ocean. . . . And then as she felt herself guided by Richard Linton, his hand warm on her bare arm, she thought . . . one day, maybe, I'll read about his marriage and turn to whoever I'm with and say: *I knew him once – on a cruise. Ever such a nice gentleman. He's a Member of Parliament now, you know . . . But no side about him. I get a card every Christmas from him.*

They won thirty-five pounds at bingo and at dinner they bought the wine for the whole table.

Lying in her bunk that night Suzie said to her, "You play your cards right, you know, and it might come off. You don't want to let the fact that his father is an M.P. and well off, put you off. People are broadminded these days – and what's wrong with you? You went to the grammar school, got all those certificates and you speak proper . . . far more than what I do. Yes, I just see you as Mrs Richard Whatever."

"Linton!"

"I know. I know."

"And do stop talking about it. I want to go to sleep."

"Sorry. Course you do. And –" Suzie gave a little giggle, "– who do we think we shall be dreaming about tonight?"

"Oh dear – listen to you. Shut up, Suzie!"

"All right, my love. Just a bit of a tease. After all, we are on holiday. Can't be serious all the time. But I've got a feeling in my bones that one day soon, probably at the next port (if they grow there) he'll be buying you a bunch of jonquils and –"

"What on earth are you talking about?"

"Jonquils. Like what that fool of a young postman brought me once two years ago. You've forgotten it, haven't you? And so has he, I'll bet. Jonquils, you told me, mean – *I desire a return of affection.*"

Suzie waited for some response, but none came. After a time she turned over and lay feeling the faint rise and fall of the ship's motion under her. Then suddenly she said aloud to no one in particular but for her own satisfaction and pleasure, "I desire a return of affection. Don't miss this fabulous offer. Can never be repeated . . ." She broke off, overwhelmed by her own outburst, and lay in her bunk giggling softly to herself.

*   *   *   *

The card room was situated on the games deck on the starboard side, tucked away from the general coming and going of the cruise passengers but close to the Dolphin Room and its convenient bar. Its long curved window gave a broad view partly dead forward and partly to starboard which meant, on the course that the ship was heading, to the south. Here and there were half a dozen tables, no fruit machines or pin-ball games. For these there was a separate – and highly patronized – room on the promenade deck.

Within a couple of days its patrons had sorted themselves out, formed little table groups, and – except for eating and sleeping – formed a little body unpolitic and mainly unsocial except within the confines of their room and the fellowship of their kind. All of them, of course, played for money . . . and fairly high stakes. And, apart from the need of money for the general necessities of life, they existed within certain hours as detached as eagles – or rooks – in their high eyrie or rookery. They were men of variety, men who could uncaringly afford to lose and men who regarded loss as a personal slight from the gods of chance. They were all civilized, with good manners and normally gentle natures, not unloath to be charitable were the cause on examination to prove good, and also, given an evening's winnings, prone to be generous; but far from easy to gull with some bad luck story. Bad luck times did not interest them. They had lived through many of their own.

One member of this coterie was Colonel Jack Sayers, a long-retired regular officer of Her Majesty's Service, a man plentifully endowed with this world's goods and able to enjoy them with the confidence of wealth, which had come originally from an ancestor who had been one of the founding members of the East India Company.

The colonel was also a friend of Mrs Picton, an acquaintanceship which had begun when she – then a Miss Randel – had been presented at court. She soon had become engaged and eventually married to an officer in the Brigade of Guards, a close friend of the now colonel. The two met one morning, quite by accident, at the ship's bureau where they had both gone to make a booking for a coach tour from Limassol around the southern part of Cyprus.

The colonel greeted her with friendly warmth, kissed her hand – uncaring of all the other people around – and said,

"My goodness, I wouldn't be so tactless as to try and remember how many years it's been – but you look as charming as ever. Well, well – and the bars are open, too. So let's go and have some morning sherry."

So they did. Three morning sherries, to be exact, and, while they were dealing with them, Mrs Picton learnt that the colonel was one of the coterie of card players which included James Goodbody, after which it was not difficult to bring up a subject now close to her heart and, when she persisted perhaps a little too openly with the subject, the colonel cocked a bushy right eyebrow and with a grin said, "Do I hear the sounds of an anxious mother concerned with the care of her only chick?"

"Well, my dear Jack, you know how it is. These days you can't tell who is who, and I must confess . . . well, dear Gloria seems to be very taken with him. But I ask you – a professional gambler."

"Oh, hardly. He plays the tables and that sort of thing – but he's no fool and doesn't get carried away." He laughed. "Actually, with all that he's got waiting for him, I think he's very level-headed at the tables. Bloody good, too, if you'll excuse my French. Got card sense . . . like some people have horse sense . . . spot the breeding and possibilities of some apparently half-starved hack."

"Colonel, what do you mean by all that he's got waiting for him?"

"Just that. He's got an only uncle – unmarried – who's rolling in it. Charming fellow. Eccentric as a duck with hiccups. If he's not a millionaire there's only a hair's breadth in it. Big estate, too. Everything goes to young Goodbody – entailed, or whatever it is. But I should think he's put it out of his mind. The young do, you know. To hell with the very distant future. And, anyway, Goodbody doesn't count chickens before they are hatched. He would never say anything about what the future might or will bring. He's too good a card player."

"Well, he certainly sounds as though –"

"He's got his head screwed on right? Well, he has. But before I go –" he reached out and took one of her hands into both his and held it fondly "– take my advice. Keep what I've told you to yourself. Don't say anything to your girl. You'll only muck things up. When he wants anyone to know he'll speak out. Agreed?"

A little grudgingly, after a pause, Mrs Picton said, "Yes . . . Oh, yes. Of course I wouldn't dream. But you are sure about all this?"

"Absolutely."

"Dear me . . . I had no idea. Of course, one could tell at once that he had breeding –"

"And common sense as well as card sense. All he's got at the moment are the cards in his hand. . . . Play them and wait to see what you draw from the shoe later. Sensible bloke. Now, my dear, not a word from you to anyone – and that includes that charming daughter of yours. After all, his uncle might marry again and have children . . . a direct heir. Not impossible . . . he's only in his sixties and as fit as a flea. The Goodbodys are notoriously long lived – but the odds for that have changed a bit these days . . . car crashes, airplane disasters, bomb going off in your favourite emporium . . . always liked that word . . . comes from the Greek, *emporion* – a trading station . . . *emporos* . . . a wayfarer or trader . . . and to take it further back –"

"Don't bother, you dear man." Mrs Picton rose and the colonel stiffly and politely followed suit. "And I certainly shall say nothing to my girl. I believe in letting human nature take its course . . . but naturally only between people of a like kind and station. I've seen too many girls marrying below them and dragging drearily around like ducks with a broken wing. Do you remember, for instance that awful Nancy Rawlings who –"

"Shall never forget her, my dear," said the colonel. "Lovely to have had a chat with you. But must be off. Give my regards to . . ." He moved away . . . his parting words diminishing in volume as he went.

119

Nice man, she thought, remembering a time when the possibility of becoming his wife had been close and dependent on her and she had turned him down . . . oh, nicely, and without breaking a friendship. Still . . . if she could arrange it between her daughter and this James Goodbody – well . . . why not? Good family . . . a bit too fond of the green-baize table but he had his head screwed on properly. And what man was ever perfect? Additionally, too, she thought – she would not over-push Gloria. Let her make up her mind irrespective of mundane financial or social prospects. True love . . . ah . . . ah.

SEVEN

LYING IN THEIR bunks in the early morning, sunlight streaming through the portholes, the faint throb of the ship's engines now mute as they lay at anchor off Athens, Suzie said, "You interested in all these ruins and things? You know, the old Greeks and all that stuff. And then there's the Parthen-something like what they told us about in the lecture the other day."

"I'd like to see it."

"It's a long climb up. No lift. And a lot of ruins at the top."

"It's one of the cradles of civilization."

"Oh, I say. Where did you get that one from? As though I didn't know. Maybe there'll be some rare rock plants at the top, too. You can take them back and propagate them."

"Shut up."

"Shan't. I feel like a chat. There's an hour before breakfast yet. I must say, I like breakfast. 'Smatter of fact I like every meal on board and do you know why?"

"Because you're putting on weight and don't look a skinny Lizzy any more?"

"I ignore that. And anyway, the answer is – because I don't have to do a damn thing about it. Just go down sit down, order and then eat it when it comes. You know something?"

"What?"

"My menfolk are no fools. That's what they've been getting for years. Well – they're going to notice the change."

"How?"

"I'm going to get married."

"Who to?"

"I haven't decided."

"But you got to be in love first."

"Nonsense. That comes last. Pick somebody you fancy, make sure he's in a good job, and has all the right parts like two legs . . . two arms . . . and the rest of it – and what is there to worry about?"

"He might turn out to be a real pig."

"So what? I can handle that. I've been doing it for years with my lot. What do you want me to do – wait till Mr Right comes along?"

"You could give it a try."

"No deal. I don't care if he's got two heads and a nice smile."

"You mean smiles."

"Ah, yes, of course, so I do. And what about you?"

"What about me?"

"Has Cupid wasted a dart on you? Ha, ha! I should think not."

"I've been invited down to stay with him and his sister at his nursery this summer."

"You'll have to watch the sister. They get very protective about brothers – no woman's ever good enough for them. Not that I care like that, though. But in your case it's different. You're both daft in a quiet way about one another. And I'm very happy for you both."

"You're running ahead a bit too fast."

"Oh, no I'm not. The way your eyes light up and his when you see one another. Even across the restaurant table . . . I don't think you know there are other people sitting around it." She sighed. "It must be lovely to be like that. But, of course, there are disadvantages. It's not only that you don't notice the people around you . . . you most of the time don't even notice what you're eating. Like sitting on a drifting cloud. Which is all very well, of course, until it begins to rain and you find the cloud getting smaller and smaller under you until it disappears."

Lily laughed. "You wait until it happens to you."

"I'll deal with it. But whoever it is – he'll get a bit of a rough time from my family lot." Suzie sat up on her bunk and began to do stretching exercises, reaching down with her arms and touching her toes, saying as she did so, "You're lucky. You can eat what you like and as much as you like and you always stay the same. If I take an extra helping of anything at the lunch buffet table or give myself a treat of chocolates or something like that between meals I blow up like a balloon."

"Nonsense."

"Well, that's how it feels. You're lucky. I don't know how you do it. You eat . . . well, like a horse almost and nothing happens. It's a bit unfair, really."

Lily laughed and said, "Is it? Things even up. You can play the piano by ear – but I can't. I couldn't play a penny whistle if I had all the lessons in the world. And that's all for the good. We don't all want to be the same, do we?"

"I suppose not. And we're not. You've only got to look around this lot aboard. Unless we've a pair of identical twins aboard we're all different from one another. And a good job we are, I suppose. Take that John Christopher, for instance. I've never met a one like him before – have you?"

"In what way?"

"Well, he's odd. Well, nice odd. But all the same odd. Don't you think so?"

"Maybe – but this whole ship is full of odd people. So's the whole world, I suppose. We all go about thinking we're normal and the rest are just a little or a lot off balance. But we're all odd, you know."

"Yes, but some people are odder than others. You take that John Christopher, for instance. He's nice but he's as mad as a coot."

"What's a coot?"

"I don't know. But it's something my brothers say. What does it matter what it is? It's mad according to them.

Anyway John Christopher is mad ... nice mad. And mysterious."

"How mysterious. You mean he's a spy, or something?"

"Course not. But he's what I call a popper-upper. You know one of those people when you think you're all alone suddenly say from behind you – *Well, me dear, how are you?* – and you jump half out of your skin. Also he's not so simple minded as he'd like people to think. I'll bet you that in war time he'd be just the kind to risk his life behind the enemy lines as a spy – and really enjoy doing it. Oh, there are plenty like that. My dad 'as a chum who spent two years in Occupied France during the war and loved every minute and he had about as much French as I've got ... Well, as I've got Welsh."

In one of the outer cabins some way forward of the girls' cabin on the port side Mrs Nancy Bell was seated in front of her dressing-table mirror, dressed and ready for breakfast and now putting on her lipstick, when there came a knock at her door. She smiled to herself, knowing perfectly well who it would be and, as she had done for some mornings now, she had already put up the lock catch so that the door could be opened from the outside. A glance at her wrist watch told her – as she knew it would – that it was half-past eight. He was always punctual and even though he had long left the army he liked to live by a routine. In some way, she thought, he drew comfort and assurance by knowing more or less what was coming next in life. A solitary, settled man of no great imagination but – and this weighed significantly with her – a man as dependable in his habits as he was with his virtues and little quirks of character. It was a pity, she had long known, that he had no high opinion of himself as a soldier, a man of war and action. Some people are born heroes – others are content to read about them and become like them only in the comfort of their daydreams. What he did not know – and what many, many more men than one would imagine didn't know – was that there wasn't a man living who, given the right time, place and hard spurring, wasn't a hero. She liked him, was fond of him, perhaps in love with him – but then, at her age she was prepared to settle for high friendship in the place of love . . . who could tell what changes time might bring?

"Come in," she called.

The door swung open and Frank Langton came in. He gave her a smile and a good-morning, then crossed to her and, in his old-fashioned way, which she liked, took her hand and, raising it to his lips, kissed it. A small thing but a gesture she loved and, had he followed it with a blunt request for her hand in marriage she would have given it with joy. She prayed that one day it would happen. She didn't care under what circumstances . . . so long as it happened. But goodness alone knew what it would take to bring him to the starting line and then to take off when the race began. She could have prompted him, of course, or have tangled him up in some seemingly at first matter-of-fact conversation which she could have subtly switched towards the point and finally left him with a wide, easy lead in to the main subject – but that was not what she wanted. He had to find his own way to come to her and ask her, since if he could not do that then there would always be some flaw in their relationship . . . some weakness which with time would betray them both. No, what she wanted from him was a declaration and a proposal which came entirely from him . . . that at least, surely every woman was entitled to expect.

Stepping back from her he smiled and said, "It's a lovely morning. We've just dropped anchor off Piraeus."

"What's that?"

"Well, it's the port for Athens. We can't berth alongside . . . so we have to go ashore in the ship's launches."

"Are there some nice things to see?"

"I don't know about Athens itself . . . just a pleasant town, I suppose. But there are plenty of Greek antiquities. The Parthenon and other classical remains."

She wrinkled up her nose and said, "Oh, I think I could do without them."

125

"Well, it's all a matter of taste, isn't it? They were great fighters, you know, the Greeks. They had to be to keep their place in the world. Soldiering in those days was a grim business. . . . Anyway, about going ashore: I took the liberty of getting us two tickets for a coach ride first to the Parthenon, then for a drive round Athens itself with time for shopping and then back to Piraeus and so aboard in one of the launches. And there's no hurry because the tour doesn't start until after lunch."

"That all sounds very nice. Are you interested in all these Greek antiquities?"

He shrugged his shoulders, and then with a grin said, "Well, not really. I mean, not to the extent of going into it all . . . I mean the history and so on. Coming up through Italy during the war there were a lot of places and things one could have seen . . . but somehow I never seemed to get round to it. 'Course I regret it now."

"Well, it's all still there. You could go and see it any time you wanted to." She gave him a brief smile and said, "Maybe if you asked me nicely I'd come with you . . ."

She marked the beginning of embarrassment in him and to save him from his own awkwardness she added quickly, "Which do you like best? The pictures or the statues or the old buildings or what?"

Without hesitation he said, "The pictures . . . I've got a book with reproductions of some of the old paintings in it. Marvellous they are. It must be wonderful to have a gift . . . you know . . . to draw or paint or to make sculptures . . . like that – what was his name? – Michael Angelo chap. But there's nothing like that in me. In fact –" he gave her a thin, almost pathetic smile, and went on, "– there's very little in me that's out of the ordinary. That's why I've never been able to ask you . . . Oh, well, never mind." He drew himself up into a stiff military manner and ran on, "Come on now – let's go and have some breakfast."

For a moment or two she felt like persisting, knowing this was the nearest he had ever come to talking intimately with her, but some instinct told her that it would be a mistake. The freedom he sought to be able to talk naturally and sincerely to her had to be found for himself without help from anyone else. She knew what he wanted and she knew that he wanted it without the benefit of help from anyone else . . . a rare pride he possessed forced that upon him.

EIGHT

ON THE FOURTH day after leaving Gibraltar the S.S. *Andreas* reached Limassol on the island of Cyprus. Since she could not lie alongside the quay, she let go her port anchor and lay moored some way well off the quayside so that her own ship's boats had to be lowered from their davits to ferry shore-going parties who wished to make a coach tour of the southern part of the island, or to spend their time exploring and shopping in Limassol itself.

Four or five coaches waited to take the ship's sightseers, and it was remarkable how many not so long ago strangers managed by no accident at all to find themselves sitting either together or within eye or hand contact with one another. The unseen minions of Eros had worked hard and invisibly. They always did with cruising parties, whether on shipboard or ashore. But in a few instances they had found their tasks done for them.

Captain Frank Langton sat alongside Mrs Bell. *His* Nancy, as he thought of her, though he would never have revealed this to her unless under some strong compulsion whose nature he could not possibly imagine; which was a little surprising, seeing that when it came to inventing wartime acts of his own heroism he had no difficulty in finding words. How often he regretted having, right from the start of meeting her, made himself out to be far, far more than he was! Behind his tall tales and bluff, robust exterior lay a thin, unprepossessing shadow of a man . . . haunting him, never leaving him, and invisible to everyone . . . except that sitting beside him now, proud of the fine figure he made

even in casual clothes, was Mrs Bell. She knew him so well
. . . thoroughly enough to be able to guess what was going
through his mind at times, recognizing the small signs of
strain when he knew discomfort from his own timidity.
Because of this she leaned closer to him and said "Frank, my
dear man . . . one of the ladies I met in the hairdressing
salon, who's been on this cruise and done this tour before,
told me about it."

"Oh, yes . . ."

"Well, there's one place they stop . . . on a high cliff. It's
got some name like Neptune's leap . . . looking over the sea.
Well I know how you are about heights – so, if you wanted to
you could stay in the coach or just wander off the road away
from the cliff. I shan't mind. The lady who told me said she
couldn't bear it . . . though it's nothing really and –"

"All right, Nancy, my dear. Don't worry about me. I can
take things as they come. Fear of heights . . . giddiness . . .
it's all in the mind, you know. I'll admit I have to brace
myself a bit more than most . . : but there you are." But, he
told himself, there was no question of 'but there you are'.
There he would never be. Deep within him, for ever part of
his nature, lurked fears . . . probably, he thought bitterly,
among them some fears which had not yet shown themselves. He could imagine them as though they were a row of
little red devils with swishing spiked tails watching him,
waiting for some situation which they could manoeuvre into
a challenge to him which would leave him powerless to find
one single brave move to match any of his so-ready bold
words. In that moment he wished he had pleaded sickness
and never come on this tour. And there wasn't any doubt
about it . . . the bloody driver was going much too fast round
the coastal road bends and corners. Damned foreigners . . .
hadn't got enough sense to know when they were doing
something dangerous. There was a big British Army
presence here, he knew . . . keeping the peace and maintain-
ing the border line in the north of the island where the Turks
were in occupation. Funny things, politics and diplomacy

... Turks in the north, Brits in the south and the true inhabitants just sitting back and accepting it all. Well, it took all sorts . . . that was what life was all about . . . taking all kinds and letting them sort themselves out. It happened between nations and it happened between individuals. Things got settled one way or another . . . *jaw, jaw* or *war, war* . . . that's what the old bulldog Churchill had said.

So he sat with Mrs Bell at his side and listened to the tour guide, a young woman with a good command of English who stood up front alongside the coach driver and gave them a running commentary on the places they passed and answered any questions the sightseers put to her. Watching her, only part-listening, he found himself wondering, when they came to the end of the tour, how much he should give her as a tip . . . for herself and the driver, of course. He fussed a bit over the problem. One didn't want to appear mean by not giving enough but on the other hand it was stupid to overtip. As he only had English money he tried to make some comparison with what he would give at home . . . but then that wasn't satisfactory. This was going to be a long trip . . . He sat there as the coach left the flat land to the west of Limassol with its banana plantations and dried-up rivers and began silently to worry to himself. Mentally he did the driving for the man at the wheel, silently issuing instructions, cautions, sharp disapprovals . . . and now and again his whole body flexing with sudden apprehension as they took a corner far too fast – or so it seemed to him.

When eventually, far along the coast, the roads having climbed higher and higher as the land rose sheer inland from the sea, they stopped on an outswinging curve of the road where, on the seaward side, there was a small patch of open ground overlooking the sea below. The guide explained that from the sea below the fall of the cliffs was the spot where tradition had it that Aphrodite had emerged – a fully formed woman-goddess – born of the sea, taking her name from the Greek word for sea foam.

Much to Mrs Bell's surprise, Frank Langton had got out

of the coach and, as she with the other tourists followed the guide towards the cliff edge, he took her hand and went with her. As she looked up at him he said, smiling thinly, "I gotta do it. Just take my hand so's no one will notice much and I'll keep my eyes shut until –"

"Oh, Frank, are you sure you –"

"Just lead me, love. Tell me when to open my eyes."

"Oh Frank . . ."

She took his hand, making it seem as casual as possible, and then walked at the tail of the visiting group to reach the cliff edge on the fringe of the sightseers, so that he could turn away and appear casual, bored even, as though he had seen enough, without attracting attention.

They went to the edge of the cliff and the woman guide's voice rose above the distant sound of the sea and the wind which stirred it into white-fringed waves breaking on the shore below. He opened his eyes and saw the breaking waves and felt the first tremors of disquiet take him . . . knowing that they would increase and possess him entirely.

He felt her hand tighten on his and she said, smiling, "You don't have to say anything. But there's nothing you can't do if you will yourself to it."

Even in his minor distress as he approached the cliff edge and saw the waves breaking on the thin strand of beach below, he had to smile and then said to her, "That's it. It's the willing part. Trouble is my will wants one thing and I want another. They're like a couple of twins . . . always scrapping."

To his surprise she laughed and gave his hand a little shake with hers and said, "Well let them squabble. Do what you want – not what either of them want."

"You're dead right . . . dead right. Only –"

He looked down the cliffside and thought to himself . . . If she were lying down there and the only thing to do was to go down after her, what would. . . ? He suddenly shook his head and closed his eyes as though he would shut out both the picture in his imagination and the scene below him of rough cliffside and a narrow strand of beach with a lazy run of white breakers moving landwards, a stiff breeze blowing the spume like a flock of small grey-white birds.

He turned without haste and began to walk back to the coach. Mrs Bell watched him go and there was nothing she did not understand. She turned away from the sight of him and, as she looked out over the windswept sea, took her handkerchief from her bag and dabbed away the beginning of tears from the corners of her eyes. She could do it openly for the sea wind was strong and people would think it was making her eyes water.

Mrs Picton certainly had no idea that there were tears in Mrs Bell's eyes as she looked straight past her – though peripherally aware of her presence and identity – at her daughter walking with James Goodbody along the cliff crest some way to her right. It looked, she thought for a moment or two, as though they were holding hands but a few moments later she realized that this was not so for young Goodbody bent down, picked up a stone and threw it skywards out over the deserted beach. Such a nice young man! And – she was rather pleased with herself about this – clearly attracted to her daughter, so why should she interfere in any way, or even tell her girl all she now knew about Goodbody's prospects (perhaps she ought to begin to call him James now . . . certainly not Jimmy). Still, there was no need to hurry, and not her part to do so, since the two seemed naturally to be drawing together. She sighed. What it was to have all before you and a plump bank balance and a steady income . . . and better still to be young, with an inheritance to come and lucky enough to find the kind of wife who knew her way around and put a premium on good form instead of dressing like God-knew-what and being into drugs and who knows what other kind of decadent goings-on. . . ? Ah, well –

A blast on the horn of their coach gave them a signal to return to the driver, who had not left his seat, and when they had all straggled back to their places the woman guide said, "Now we take you to lovely . . . how you say? Rustic?

132

Yes . . . rustic garden café where you get wine or morning coffee and biscuits. Also many things to buy as souvenirs . . . all things made here in the countryside and in Limassol.''

They were taken about half a mile farther down the hill and then turned off up a rough road for a few hundred yards to a large café set in a little dell around which flowered magnolias and hibiscus below small clouds of hovering butterflies.

The three of them went inside and had biscuits and sweet sherry while Mrs Picton engaged James Goodbody in some polite probing about his acquaintances and gave him full marks for not bringing out the fact of his uncle in any of his responses. In fact, she thought, the more she got to know him the more worthy and suitable a young man to marry her daughter he seemed to be – and James Goodbody, reading her thoughts with the ease which sometimes he could read the overall worth of a player's bridge hand by the changing weather of the man's face, was amused and polite. From somewhere he was sure, she had got wind of his uncle – a tight-fisted, unpredictable, amusing, unstable enigma of a man as likely – had his estate not been entailed – to have left all he owned to a dog's home – where perhaps, he thought wryly at this moment, it would do far more good than he was likely to do with it. But, at least, he would like to have the chance to compete on fair terms for it. Fat chance though – the old boy rated dogs higher than human beings.

At this moment Mrs Picton said, ''Now I wonder where that daughter of mine has wandered off to? She's got no bump of location at all, you know. James. Do be a good man and go and find her. The coach leaves in about ten minutes and she's probably wandered off collecting plants. Her sponge bag is full of them almost already, but half of them will be dead before she gets them home. It's the way she is . . . starts full of enthusiasm and then after a while she begins to lose interest . . . what she needs of course is something . . . or some one . . . that absolutely captures her interest and imagination, because I have to say that once she does get

133

really interested there's no stopping her . . . she just goes on and on and on. When she falls in love, really in love, and marries, the lucky man will have in his loving care a jewel beyond all price and —"

"I'm sure he will. You wait there, dear Mrs Picton, and I'll go and find her." He gave her a large reassuring smile and went out of the café.

Quite a few of the members of the coach party were strolling around among the flowering shrubs, admiring the blooms, but he could see no sign of Gloria. Then a voice at his side said, "If you're looking for Miss Picton she went up the little valley path a little while ago . . . collecting flowers, it looked like."

"Oh, thank you," said James.

As he walked quickly off, Suzie Wilson said to Lily Franklin, "You can always tell, can't you?"

"Tell what?" asked Lily.

"When someone's in love. You can feel a sort of vibration coming out of them. 'Course with men it's sort of pitched lower and slower and if you've got an ear for it there's no way they can hide it. You ever noticed that?"

"I can't say I have."

"Funny . . . I get it from you very often. Just after you've seen or talked with —"

"All right — we won't go any further with that. 'Course you could always set up as a fortune teller . . . have a little stall in your front garden . . . your father and the lads could tout for custom — particularly if they've got good ears for vibrations."

At this they both laughed and the coach driver blew a couple of blasts on his horn to call the party together.

Two hundred yards up the narrow valley, a gulley washed out by the seasonal rains and its sides thick with bougain-villaea growths and other shrubs, the path took a sharp right-hand bend. As James Goodbody walked round this he heard a woman's half-shout, half-scream and he knew it was from Gloria. He ran forward around the projecting spur of a large bank of pink broom growths to find her standing in the

134

middle of the rough path held by a man with his arms around her tightly and his face thrust forward at hers in an attempt to kiss her which she was avoiding by turning away from him.

In the few moments which it took Goodbody to reach them small details etched themselves into his memory . . . a bunch of wild grasses and flowers which Gloria had collected lying part scattered on the path . . . the man's face over her shoulder as he sought to kiss her and the constraining but caressing movement of his hands across and down her back . . . a little black velvet hat she wore which in the stress of these moments even reminded Goodbody of the Boy's Brigade uniform at home of his uncle's bailiff's son. . . . Then there was nothing to note in him except a swift, roaring rage of anger and fury and a great inarticulate cry issuing from his mouth as though he had turned animal as he leapt forward, seized the man's wrist from the hold he had round Gloria's waist and with a vicious upward swing freed it from her as the man stepped sideways and his right hand dropped to his waist to pull from his sash a long, bone-handled, curving dagger. Before the man could move completely around Gloria to attack him, Goodbody jumped for him. His right fist slammed into the man's face, hard-stubbed with more than a day's growth of beard, driving him backwards from Gloria.

But he held his balance and now came for Goodbody, pushing Gloria aside as he passed her. Right hand holding the dagger high, his face gleaming with sweat, his eyeballs moving in a fast flicker and with a great grunt of anger and rage he lunged at Goodbody. But by now the fury in Goodbody had been sharply controlled and the experience of many a past fight at school and during Army service and amateur boxing stood him in good stead. As the man came forward on his lunge Goodbody stepped back and aside and the blade swept downwards six inches short of his left shoulder and side. Goodbody knocked the knife out of the man's grasp with the firm edge of his left hand and at the same time crossed a right swing to his face, catching him on the side of the chin and sending him sprawling into the soft bulk of a broom patch where he lay, gasping and panting and obviously not eager for more fight.

Without looking at her, his eyes on the man, wary of any movement he might make, he said sharply to Gloria, "Get on down the path. The coach is waiting. Tidy as you go. I'll follow – but I want you away first."

Without a word she moved past him and, his eyes never leaving the man, he waited until he knew she was well down the pathway. From the ground the man said something to him in his own language which meant nothing to him and then, cautiously stood up and, with a sudden burst of activity, turned and ran up the pathway. Without hurry Goodbody made his way down the pathway to the waiting coach. As he took his seat somebody unseen behind him in the rear of the coach said aloud, "Funny . . . there's always somebody who keeps everybody else waiting on a coach trip . . ."

And as the coach moved off Mrs Picton turned round in her seat and said to Goodbody. "Thank you, James. I'm afraid my dear daughter has little sense of time."

He smiled and answered, "Oh, I don't know – she was on her way back when I met her. Anyway . . . don't they say, if you're young and beautiful and a woman you can be excused for keeping someone waiting?"

"Don't tell her that. She's bad enough already."

"Oh, no . . . I think –" He broke off suddenly.

"You think what, James?"

He grinned. "Well . . . that . . . well, never mind and –"

Gloria looked across at her mother, and said sharply, "Please let it go, mother. I'll tell you all about it later. I just want to say that James did me a great . . . well, he came to my help when I needed it."

"Indeed? How was that?"

"Mother. Later . . ."

"Oh, very well . . . though what all the mystery is about I can't think."

*   *   *   *

Mrs Chambers had wished that when they sent you on these tours they would provide you all with a little map and a list of the places to be visited with some details of their history. As it was the guide, sitting up alongside the driver, would turn to them and start talking away about the next place to be seen – and how could you carry it all in your head? Though, of course, on shipboard, in the cinema there was always beforehand a film and talk show which covered the places to be visited . . . But then everything became confused because there was far more shown in the film than you actually got to see and . . . well, anyway, she supposed, if you were really interested then you could always take one of these cultural shipboard tours with real professors and the like at hand to explain things. But that was not for her. This she was trying to explain as she sat on a grassy bank beneath the shade of an olive tree with John Christopher for company as they waited for most of the rest of the company to finish their tour of an old Crusader castle . . . a massive tower rising high above the flat plain with icecream carts and snack-bar stalls clustered in the roadway . . . nothing left of the grand Crusader castle except the tower and the exposed skeleton work of the ground-floor rooms and the cellars and great kitchen and store rooms.

She said, "You mean they came all this way from all over Europe to liberate Jerusalem . . . never did . . . and then stayed on here?"

"Some of them . . . yes."

"But why – why didn't they go back home?"

"Because they lived in hope . . . or maybe there was nothing back where they came from which called as strongly to them as their crusading fervour . . . their undiminishable hope. Or perhaps if they were young and far from being rich

137

or aristocratic they saw for themselves here more freedom and opportunity than they could have returned to. Man is always looking for something better than he already knows. Why do you think we're going into outer space? Just to know about it?"

"Why else?"

"Because hope drives us. You've heard of the *Mayflower*?"

"Oh, yes. The Pilgrim Fathers who sailed from the Barbican at Plymouth for America."

"A new land, new hopes, new starts . . . Man's always looking for these."

"New starts . . ." she sighed. "That would be nice. But why do you have to go abroad to get it?"

"You don't. There are dozens of ways and opportunities . . . always popping up. You just have to have the courage . . . maybe the common sense . . . to latch on to one of them."

Suddenly she was unexpectedly almost angry with him. He sat there giving her easy – so it seemed – talk and advice but what did he know of the . . . all right, she didn't mind using the words . . . the nitty-gritty of some people's lives? New starts. He should talk! What new start could she make? Take her husband back to the supplier and ask for a new one under the terms of the guarantee?

He said quietly. "You're angry."

Surprising herself, she answered, "Yes I am."

"With me?"

"With you, but more with the way things are. Do human beings really interest you?"

"Of course."

"Well, then, listen to this. I met a man, we fell in love with one another. Many years ago. Everything was like the promise of spring, the joy of summer and the fulfilment of autumn – It's all right –" she gave a little bitter laugh "– they're not my words. I remember them from a tear-off calendar. So, we were young, in love and the future was rosy. Do you know what will be happening in our flat tonight? Another woman will be sleeping in our bed and he won't care a damn whether I know it or not. That's my husband – that's the young man who once spelt out with a stick on the wet sands of a lonely Cornish beach these words for me – . . . *love me for love's sake, that ever more* – *Thou mayest love on, through love's eternity*. What other ears than mine have heard that from him since?"

"If I knew – what good would it do? It's not what a man does. It's what he is – or what he has strayed from being. All of us . . . we lose ourselves at times . . . or put on a masquerade . . . give ourselves licence to play another part from the one ordained by life." He smiled suddenly and put out a long thin hand and just brushed the tips of her fingers where her hand lay open on her knee and she had the brief sensation that the gentlest of electric currents flowed from him to her. Then he said, looking up towards the top of the tall ruined tower of the ancient crusader castle, "Each day hope is reborn. Only the past is fixed. Which is better – to live by something already immutable or to give yourself to the new day and the days beyond that day . . . to the future? That's where miracles occur – in the days to come, not in the days which are already consumed. But, of course, when the miracle comes not everyone always recognizes it and –"

She laughed suddenly and said brightly, "You're as good as a tonic. You really are. Though you haven't, in a way, said a thing I haven't thought for myself before."

"Good. Then set it free from your thoughts into your life."

"How?"

"Through prayer and patience. Through self-reliance and not self-pity. We all lose – and sometimes regain – things in life. Every child knows that. It happens all the time. *Do this. Don't do that. No, you can't have that. Yes, here it is, but this time take better care of it* . . . Remember – no one lives who is solely responsible for his or her sins. A world with just one person in it is unimaginable. Human sin is not redeemable unless there is potential forgiveness waiting from the one who has been sinned against. . . ." He laughed gently. "Or am I getting both you and myself mixed up a little?"

She shook her head and for a moment stretched out a hand

139

and laid it on his, feeling the warmth in it and the physical sense of a latent strength which filled her with sudden comfort. She lowered her head, to hide the near onset of tears in her eyes and stood up, saying, "Forgive me . . . but . . . but . . . I would like to walk a little by myself."

"Of course. But don't go far. The coach party will be here soon."

"Don't worry. And thank you . . ."

He watched her disappear through a bank of olive trees and so into the garden surrounding the old castle and he thought about the Christian warriors who had come from all over Europe to free the glorious city of Jerusalem from the pagan conquerors . . . leaving home, kin and, sometimes for ever, their own dear countries . . . Jerusalem from whence the Dear One, the God-given One, the sweet Jesus borne by the Holy Mary . . . and all so long ago. He said slowly to himself, 'Like a deer that longs for running streams, my soul thirsts for you . . .'

And as he sat there, elbows on his knees, hands clasped together supporting his chin, a small mongrel terrier-type dog trotted up to him and, squatting in the dust, raised its muzzle to him. Seeing it, he suddenly smiled and then laughed to himself as he reached into his jacket pocket and pulled out a small tin of sweets and gave one to the animal, saying, "Like a mongrel that longs for sweets . . . Aye, the world is full of longing . . . Like a deer that longs for running streams, my soul longs for you, my –"

He broke off as he saw the first of their main party coming out of the tower and beginning to cross towards him and the waiting coach. Watching them he smiled to himself at the way they walked . . . so many of them had formed pairings or little cliques of three or four. Very few walked alone and this was, he guessed, that just for a while they had accidentally got separated from their chosen companion or companions. Man was a social animal. Strength and security came through groupings, no matter how small. How many of the friendships made on this cruise would last, he wondered?

Probably more than most people would believe. The more complicated the world and living became the more need was growing for friendship, for associations, fewer people walked alone, loneliness was weakness, and far too easily put under threat. Together people walked and worked and lived with a warming sense of security on the whole . . . even all those years ago He had drawn His disciples to him and they had walked together until the bitter end.

The dog suddenly barked at him as though in reprimand for getting no titbit and turned and trotted off in search of fresh alms. A few moments later Lily Franklin and Suzie Wilson came up to him.

With a grin, he said, "What did you think of it?"

"Awful," said Suzie. "Like a prison and too many steps to the top rooms . . . half an hour's climb –"

"In armour!" added Lily. "Everywhere dark as a coal hole. And no sign of a bathroom. Still . . . you got to hand it to them. They could have stayed at home and lived in comfort – but they didn't."

"That's it – they didn't. Many of them brought it with them. Like the knight who had this castle built. Some were pure adventurers, of course, but most were men of great faith – *Revere the Lord, you His saints. They lack nothing, those who revere Him* –"

Suzie broke in, "*Strong lions suffer want and go hungry – but those who seek the Lord lack no blessing.*"

He stood up, stepped between them and took each of them by an arm and said, "Allow me to escort you two ladies back to the coach."

And as they went, Suzie laughed and said, "I liked the way you spoke then. You know you should have been a parson. You'd have had all the ladies of the parish dancing attendance on you."

He grinned. "Alas, alas – that I didn't think of that."

"So what do you do?" asked Suzie.

"I'm a salesman . . . a travelling salesman . . . in my father's business. And –" Just then the hooter of their coach

141

blasted three times and drowned his words as they began to hurry towards the waiting vehicle.

*　　*　　*　　*

That evening, some considerable time after dinner, while the S.S. *Andreas* moved eastwards on a calm sea, a sea almost glass-like and smooth which threw back the reflection of the stars in the cloudless sky, Lily and Richard Linton sat on deck on the port side to catch the faintest of zephyrs that cooled a little the unrelenting heat of the day.

To begin with they had sat almost in silence, content with one another's company, watching with idle eyes the passing of deck strollers making their after-dinner promenade . . . out now for fresh air and the pleasure of walking with always the great rolling sweep of the sea stretching into the darkening distance of the vast spread of the Mediterranean. Food they had had and entertainment by the cabaret afterwards . . . now, below deck, the restaurant was full with the second sitting and soon they too would be taking their places for the second showing of the cabaret.

Quite out of the blue, surprising Lily, Richard Linton said, "I know you live with your aunt, and I know that fairly often you go as a temporary companion to people."

She laughed. "I wouldn't be here if I didn't. One of my 'ladies', you know, when she died left me a little money and also paid for all the expenses of this cruise."

"I'm not surprised. You must have been a very good companion."

"I don't know about that. But she was a very lovely old lady – and a very intelligent and well-read one. Particularly about plants, too. There wasn't anything she didn't know about them."

He laughed. "That's a big statement. There's more to learn about plants than there is about human beings. Did you learn a lot about plants from her then?"

"Yes. She had a big garden, a lovely greenhouse and a

142

gardener who pretended always to be bad tempered when he was – underneath – the nicest sort of person in the world."

"That doesn't surprise me." He laughed, "We're all like that."

"You speak for yourself."

"Oh, but you agree, don't you?"

"No comment."

"Oh, dear – that puts me off a bit. Still, I can take it. Now tell me about this language of flowers she taught you."

"Why?"

"Because I could use it. You see, I've got a big nursery garden. Well, big for me. I employ three men and run the garden shop by myself except for help three times a week from my aunt."

"Is she interested in plants?"

"Not the slightest. She says it just keeps her from getting too bored on her own. I can't think why – she's a member of all sorts of committees, hunts twice a week in season, teaches deaf-and-dumb classes and is a member of the county council and various committees. She's a marvellous woman. Her fiancé lost his life in submarines during the war and she's never married. She says quite openly and cheerfully – God brought us together, God parted us. Not ours to question why. In the fulness of time on this earth or our next resting place we shall perhaps understand why. . . . But let's come back to this language of flowers."

"I know why you want to know. You don't fool me." Lily laughed. "You're not some unsophisticated country type . . . happy as the day is long in your glasshouses and garden plots. People will buy more readily if there's a little label stuck in the pot giving the flower message . . . *Affection beyond the grave . . . Consumed by love . . . pleasures of memory . . . your qualities like your charms are unequalled.*"

"Well, they are."

"Balderdash!"

"What a gorgeous word. I had an uncle who used it.

Anyway what's wrong with using whatever gimmick works in order to sell things?"

"Nothing – so long as it's a good article at a fair price."

"No trying to put one over on the public. An indifferent lot of tulip bulbs . . . plants that have been overforced – but who's to know?"

"The customer is in time – and then you'll see him once when he comes to complain and tick you off – and then never again."

He was silent for a while, just looking at her, half-smiling, half-pensive, then said, "Well, of course, you could choose whichever you wanted to. It would be your choice."

For a moment or two she was silent, a puzzled frown on her forehead, her eyes on him now taking small gleams of starlight reflected upwards from the fast darkening sea. Then she said, "What choice?"

"Choices, actually."

She laughed. "You're leaving me behind. I'm not with you at all. What is all this?"

He grinned. "I thought women were supposed to know instinctively."

"To know what?"

"Oh, dear – you really mean that you are not with it?"

For a moment almost crossly, she answered, "I not only mean that I'm not really with it, but if you don't make yourself clear very quickly then you'll find yourself sitting alone here. And what's more . . . if it's some kind of joke or what-have-you then I can tell you that you've picked a very poor evening for it 'cause I'm sitting here as near in a way to paradise and so on than I've ever been in my life and I'm in no mood for conundrums or riddle-me-re questions."

To her surprise she saw his face change from its slightly teasing, smiling mood to an almost half-witted, slack mouthed, dumb-dog chastised look; and almost stuttering the words, he said, "Oh, Lord . . . I . . . I . . . I didn't mean to upset you – but I wanted to come to the point in sort of stages because –"

144

She smiled then, her own instinct, which had been budging her, now fully in charge and making no mistake about their message.

She said, "Why don't you forget the stages? Go right to the point." She laughed then, all her instincts fully active, all her womanly prescience harmoniously in tune and, overall, the star-silvered dark velvet canopy of the sky lacking only the moon for the stage to be properly set.

He stood up and said, almost like a small boy asking permission to leave the room, "Would you promise to stay right here while I walk right round the deck? Please?"

"Will that help?"

He grinned then and said, "Well, if it doesn't I'll jump overboard."

"Now you're playing on my sympathy. I suggest you start walking because I can't wait for you to get back. And don't think for a moment that I've been fooled. Go on. I'll be here."

She sat down on the edge of the nearest sunbathing bed and stared out over the deck rails at the star-crystalled sky. There should have been a moon, but either it had come and gone in daylight or its night visit was still long distant. Of course, they had both known it and that at some time it would be spoken . . . though how to put such a thing in words that really explained it was something beyond them. There were times when she was sure that she had known it was all there right from the first moment of meeting . . . how could one be sure . . . how could one trust to the truth of a memory which carried no certificate of authenticity?

He came back eventually and sat on the edge of the deck sunbed beside her and, taking her right hand in his, said, "I know we haven't known each other for very long, but I can't help that and I hope it's the same for you because surely there must be times when two people know at once what's happening – though, of course, it's obviously quite as genuine when it takes a much longer time. It's all, I suppose, a question of character and temperament. Like, for instance,

I suppose the way a Scottish Highland shepherd would handle it naturally couldn't be the same as the way, say, a Welsh postman would."

Silently enjoying herself, seeing the easy everyday assurance of demeanour that was normally his now being demolished in the turbulence of his feelings, she took – as every woman when sure of herself and her position had a right to – time out to be oblique before coming apparently to heel and docilely mouthing the appropriate responses. Not that she didn't love him. She did. Or at least, if she didn't, then something very odd was happening to her to which she could give no known name. She loved him. As simply as that. But she was not to be easily won.

She said, "Of course not. A Highland shepherd and a Welsh postman are more different than chalk and cheese. They live different lives so they think differently about a lot of things."

Quite abruptly, almost challenging, he said, "Well, what do you think about me?"

"I don't know. What do you want me to think about you?"

"Well, we get on, don't we?"

" 'Course we do. That's why we're sitting here having a conversation that would sound daft to most people and, I've got to say it, seems to be getting nowhere fast and so –"

He made her break off by raising his right hand as though he were a traffic controller halting all onward progress, and said severely, but his eyes smiling, "Ha . . . Now I get it. You're playing with me. Cat and mouse?"

"Rubbish. I'm sitting here enjoying your company – and not understanding why you're beating about the bush so much. Why don't you come to the point?"

He was silent for a while, clearly surprised, and then gave a little laugh and said, "I knew it . . . I don't know why. But when I first began to know you I sensed there was something about you that . . . well, that sort of told me that . . . well that we were sort of the kind that . . . well, the kind that . . . that . . ."

Smiling, she helped. "That sort of . . . well sort of . . . Oh, dear, you may be good with plants. I'm sure you are. But you're not much good with words."

"No. I know I'm not. And I don't mind you teasing me about it. But I have got something which makes up for it all."

"Oh?"

"Yes. I know what I want and I know where I'm going." He stood up, and went on, "I'm going to have one of the finest nursery gardens in our part of the world. I've got my eye on it already. And there's a site there where I shall build a house that will be apart and secluded yet near to the whole set-up."

She looked at him, liking his seriousness but hoping that it would never really take him over completely. Enough was enough. And she said, "And then you'll marry and have children . . . expand to other gardens . . . become a tycoon – I've often wondered about that word and dear Suzie always calls it typhoon. Not because she doesn't know better – but because it's the kind of thing she likes to do. Shall I tell you something about Suzie? She's better educated than you could imagine . . . well, from the way she speaks sometimes. But she's a great reader – always got a book propped-up as she cooks or sews or knits – and the radio going! And she soaks it all in and never forgets – though sometimes if it's convenient she pretends to. She's the kind you want for your nursery garden shop. Why don't you ask her? She'd love to get away from those brothers of hers."

He grinned then and said, "Well – thanks for the tip. Perhaps if other things I have in mind don't come off . . . well, then I might have a word with her."

*   *   *   *

It was late, past midnight, but the night air was warm and there was no more wind than an occasional zephyr. They sat close together, in separate deck chairs adjusted to the limit of their upright position. Over her knees he had tucked around

147

her a small plaid blanket which someone had left on the nearby sunbathing couch. They had just sat conscious of the easy, happy flow of the evening . . . dinner, now long finished, but which had had that evening a menu full of Cockney rhyming slang. Some good, some bad; but none which was unacceptable and enhanced not a little by the wine at table. And now some hours later, with coffee and liqueurs recently behind them, and he conscious that he should be soon finding his way to the gaming table but uniquely and not unpleasantly not caring a damn whether he went or not. Indifferent, not from drink, but from a new-sprung growth of spirit which reached back to the drama of the island tour and the assault on the young lady who now sat at his side. Full content, one hand reached out less to hold than to caress the back of her right hand as it lay on the chair arm, he sang very quietly, the sound encompassed between them, cradled but stirring and marked now and then by her small, almost breathless laugh . . . a sigh, a single bright note and, often with a caressing soft giggle from her . . .

Put on your Almond Rocks and Daisy Roots.
Put on your Oxford Scholar and Peckham Rye.
Put on your Tit for Tat and take a Ball of Chalk
Down the Frog and Toad to the Rub a Dub Dub for a Pig's Ear.

It had all come, he told himself, from the Cockney dinner menu that evening.

Now they were seeing how much they could remember, laughing, his arm reached out and she lightly holding his left hand in one of hers.

"Bells of St Helen?"

"Easy," he said. "Chilled Sliced Melon. Loop the Loop?"

"Clear Soup. And I like this one." She giggled gently and he thought it was one of the most exciting sounds he had ever heard. "Lilian Gish."

"Fried Fish. Kate and Sidney?"

"Steak and kidney. Catch a thief?"

"Roast beef. Duke of York?"

148

"Roast pork . . . I don't know about my mother."

"Why not?"

"One moment she warns me against you . . . night hawk, big gambler, one of the never-settle-down ones and then –"

"She has second thoughts. And I did save you from a fate worse than death."

"Personally, just at the moment, I can't think of any fate worse than death . . . What, leave all this . . . sailing across the Mediterranean, the air balmy, the sky a blaze of stars, music coming softly from somewhere and beside me . . . well . . . do I have to say more? . . . Now, just be serious and answer some questions."

"I've done all that. I told you. From now on I'll be earlier to bed and I'll get myself a job. My uncle will like that."

"Well let's stick with this. What kind of job can you do?"

"You'd be surprised."

"Then surprise me. I know you are going to come into money when your uncle goes. Mamma always knows all about that kind of thing. But I want to know what my husband does or wants to do."

"Shall I let you into a secret?"

"If you think it will help."

"I'm not sure of that. But the honest fact is I don't know what I want to do. I've tried a lot of things in a half-hearted way but I've always come back to . . . well, to what you know I am."

"You like risks and calculating as near as you can the odds for and against things. That's adventuring?"

"I wouldn't argue against that. And where would the world be today if it hadn't been for its adventurers?" He pointed to the stars overhead. "They're up there now, you know . . . making new frontiers for man. But I'm too old for that lark."

"What lark aren't you too old for?"

He laughed. "This is like the Spanish Inquisition. If you've got enough money or can make it in a pleasant fashion . . . why torture yourself with an uneasy conscience

149

because so many others can't do it your way? Life is like that."

"The disciples gave up everything and followed Christ."

"Well, so they did. But I think that's going a bit beyond the limit. So, I make money gambling. Is that a great sin?"

"No, I don't think so – though plenty do. But I tell you something which I would like to make quite clear between us."

"Now what? And we're not even engaged yet!"

He laughed and she laughed with him and she took his hand and held it, kneading the back of his knuckles caressingly, and said, "I want to be proud of you. Proud that you can have something you can point to and say – That's mine. I did it. That's what I do – and there's nothing else in the world just like it."

"Well, I'll go for that if I can find anything that fits the bill."

He stood up, put his hands on her shoulders and, pulling her up and gently to him, kissed her.

As she stepped back from him, she said, "That was nice."

He grinned. "I know. None of your mass produced nonsense."

"Oh, I knew that." She blew a kiss to him and then turned and walked away and left the deck, going into the Peacock Room, from which came the faint sounds of orchestral music. He knew what she would do. Sit and think, the music weaving into her thoughts and he told himself that finding her, falling in love with her could almost seem to be ordained because he had long known he was on the point of change, the point of dissatisfaction with himself.

He sat down and lit himself a cigarette, one of the very few he smoked each day . . . and lucky, he thought wryly, if he would be allowed that liberty when married. He whistled very gently between his teeth and between the luxury of drawing at his cigarette, a snatch or two from *When a Man Marries his Troubles Begin*. Then he thought . . . well, not really. His own father and mother had clearly known happiness. And so had he. Oh, he bulked out his income with gambling, and successfully. His uncle took no umbrage at that way of life. You must do what you can best do at the moment. He'd been lucky. And could be luckier . . . let's face it there was his uncle with his wealth and estate and all to come to him. What was he doing now but marking time until the gates of the promised land opened.

A voice above him said, "I'll give you sixpence for them, too much of course but that's only because I haven't got a penny."

John Christopher, as though he had materialized rather than made human progression to it, sat down on the edge of the sun-bathing bed facing him, saying, "It's too good a night to go to bed. We miss a lot in our sleep."

"Except dreams."

"Oh dear . . . dreams. Yes. But tell me – if you had the choice now given to you never to dream again in sleep – would you take it?"

"I don't think so. The best card hands I've ever held have been in my dreams. And I've backed outsiders that have romped home. And I've gone to dinner parties or whatever where I've talked and behaved brilliantly and seen the admiration in people for me. Lovely stuff. But then –"

"One wakes up?"

"True."

"But you're not very keen on waking up, are you?"

"No idea what you mean. But –" he gave a broad smile "– if it's the beginning of a lecture, don't worry. Just carry straight on. I'm used to it. Some time or other everyone I get friendly with or close to thinks they should take me in hand and wean me from what they regard as my idleness . . . or feckless way of living. And why? Because I live, eat well or badly, smile or frown . . . one year can only make it as far as Cannes and another treat myself to Acapulco and two weeks trekking in the Andes. I don't ask for anything. I take what comes."

"Which is quite a lot . . . I mean your uncle."

Goodbody grinned. "Oh, he's a great scout – but I wouldn't depend on him. He's more than likely to marry again and father a son. Besides I don't like thinking of people as Christmas crackers – when the tug comes what's going to drop out for me?" He paused for a moment, and then with a firm edge of frankness, went on, "You're a great one, aren't you, for going round stirring people up and getting them to talk. Nothing wrong with it so long as they respond willingly. But what do you get from it?"

"Wisdom."

"That doesn't fetch much on the market these days. Do it – don't read about it. That's – with a few obvious prohibitions – the best way to get on in this world. What I want to know is what you *really* get from making friends and influencing them. It's something like that, isn't it? Missionary work, perhaps?"

The other laughed. "No. I just like people and asking them questions. I suppose I get it from my father. Roughly speaking I suppose he knew that all the answers have existed since . . . well, Adam and Eve left the garden. The real problem is to find the right question to fit the answer you already know."

Goodbody laughed and said, "Oh, no – you don't catch me like that. I was brought up on Alice in Wonderland. *'It's a poor sort of memory that only works backwards,' the Queen remarked.* That's in a sense why I'm a good card player. Mine works forward. So does every professional mind. A tennis champion sees the end of the stroke as he shapes to play it. All men and women of true genius are given the gift of reading . . . foreseeing the future. Some see farther into it than others. Some have clearly seen and foretold the day and manner of their death. Our great Saviour for instance."

"You are a religious man?"

"But, of course. Every true card player is. Destiny deals the hands. There's no such thing as pure chance. Man – my father used to say – is shaped by two things . . ." he laughed, ". . . his eye-colouring and compassion from his mother and all the rest from his father . . . one the great glory of colour and creation and the other the strength and hardiness of the tiller of fields and the raiser of the great stone spires of places of worship in which God's love and compassion towards men could be celebrated with eternal thanksgiving . . . Now –" he laughed a little self-consciously "I've got a pack of cards in my pocket. Would you like a game of Beggar my Neighbour?"

John Christopher laughed and shook his head.

"You disapprove of gaming?"

"No. Chance moves among men like a breeze through a wood. Chance and the wind are eternal. We must abide by their vagaries."

"And faith?"

"Faith is our passport to take us through life. One must cherish it because once lost it is not always possible to get a replacement issued to you quickly."

"You should be in the church. Sermons bore me normally, but I think you might come up with something a man could get his teeth into."

The other laughed, and said, "The picture of someone chewing away at a sheaf of sermon notes would entrance the boys in the choir, since the young know that all adults are one way or another mad. Well . . . it's been very nice talking to you. Good night."

Goodbody watched him move away down deck, then gave a shrug of his shoulders and shook his head. He was a bit touched, of course, that was clear. Probably brought up an only child . . . cosseted. Private tutor maybe. Certainly never the rough and tumble of a public school. Nice chap, though.

He stood up, glanced at his watch and saw that it was time for him to take his evening's . . . what? Recreation? Dissipation? Distraction? Opiate? Drug? Time passer . . . even waster. Not that it mattered much anyway. His fellow players were a poor selection this cruise. Something, he felt, had gone from the evening's ritual. What was it? Something that had happened to him? Then, far from suddenly, it

153

slowly came to him – *faith is our passport through life*. Good phrase of course – but what did it mean? Faith in ourself . . . or faith in others . . . or both . . . or what? Or perhaps faith in the wisdom and understanding charity of the Top Man. Without a shred of irreverence he wondered if ultimately He controlled everything from the fall of a leaf to the fall or turn-up of a card. True faith, he realized and wondered why he had never thought of it before, was like carrying a lucky rabbit's foot around with you. Without it you felt bereft of good fortune even before the cards had been dealt. With it . . . well, Hope sat on your shoulder and Lady Luck smiled at you from some far part of the room. Faith was a passport to take one through life. He smiled to himself. What a lot of crap, really. Once you started pulling ideas out of the bag you never knew what might come up. And, anyway, such thinking could only muddle the cards and his luck in the evening session. Clear the decks for action.

He stood up and began to make his way across the room and was almost at the far door leading to the port side and the short walk to the card room when, from behind him, a woman's voice said quietly, "What were you dreaming about?"

He turned to see Gloria Picton in a midnight-blue taffeta evening dress, slim-cut and very fashionable. A generously cut stole of the same material around her shoulders, the stiff folds forming an attractive frame to her long white neck, around which was the only accessory in the form of a simple but expensive string of pearls. He grinned and said, "Why you, of course."

"Tell that to the marines."

"I would if there were any aboard. But if you walk out on deck and we find a spot sheltered from the evening breeze, I'll tell you something, as they say, not to your advantage or my advantage. But to our –"

"You can skip the rest."

"All right. Let's go."

He took her arm and escorted her out on to the promenade

deck where they found two deck chairs sheltered from the still warm but now robust night breeze. They sat close together and he put his hand on hers where it rested on the end of her chair arm and said, "I don't know how good my chances are – but I'm going to risk them. But first let me say, I love you and you would do me great honour if you could say that you love me and would be my wife. I don't think I could make it any plainer than that."

She laughed. "There would have been no need."

"And your answer?"

"Oh, well – I shall have to think about that."

"Because it's been so sudden?"

"Oh, no. I knew it might come – and then that it might not – so I didn't give it close thought. Now I must."

Pleasantly, he said, "You make it sound like a business contract."

"Oh, no. It's much more important than that." The starlight and backlight from the Peacock Room behind them put a thin halo around her blonde hair and cast her face mostly in shadows, so that he could not read her mood from her expression . . . though in her voice was a positive tone of teasing. "Of course, you must know that I love you . . . or, at least am very, very close to loving you. After all you saved me from a fate worse than death and –"

"Oh, scrub that."

"You mean any man would have done that to rescue me?"

"Of course."

"Well, I suppose so – so it doesn't make it very remark-able –" her eyes shone with starlight as she teased him "– does it? You just happened to be there. But it might well have been the coach driver."

"But you wouldn't marry him."

"I might once I got to know him. He's probably a student on vacation from the University of Athens and his father has a shipping fleet half as big as that of Onassis and –"

"You should write romantic novels."

She laughed. "No thanks. I'm living one. That's what all

cruises are. Romantic novels. Look at you – you hardly know me and here you are asking me if I will marry you. Don't tell me if I say no that you will throw yourself overboard?"

"I wouldn't be so damned silly."

"Ah – now there speaks the real Mr James Goodbody. Shall I tell you something about him?"

"Please do."

"You may not like it."

"Well, tell me anyway."

"How do you stand on this trip with your gambling?"

"You mean plus or minus and how much?"

"Yes."

"I'm about five hundred pounds up."

"Are you really? You clever old thing."

"So?"

"Well," she rose from her chair and stood over him, looking more beautiful than any woman he had ever seen – though he knew this couldn't be true – but it did seem so at the moment.

"Well, what?"

"Well . . . I wondered . . . and please don't be cross with me when I say this . . . I wondered why someone so obviously capable and intelligent – and nice and pleasant to be with –" for a moment to his surprise she sketched a kissing gesture towards him with her lips "– should be so content that the major thing in his life is the playing of cards. Wasn't or isn't there anything else in life you once longed passionately to do?"

"Well . . ." He looked up at her his mouth almost idiotically slack and partly open, his eyes rounded to give the final touch of inanity to his face, and then he said putting on a Somerset accent, "Well now, missus . . . Oh, yes there be. I do have a fancy to run a small country hotel . . . I got the money, so 'tis only a question of finding the right place and staff and a wife to help with the sort of things that women can do."

She grinned. "Just that. To help with things that a woman

can do. As a matter of fact you don't want anything of the kind – and you know it. You're going to inherit from your uncle – and the thing you're best at is waiting to – and I mean this respectfully – step into a dead man's shoes."

"Dear Uncle?"

"Of course. I thought about this. And I'll be frank with you and tell you why – because I love you. No – just stay where you are." She put out a hand and waved him back into his seat. "Your gambling is like a fat boy's gluttony. There's no real need for the food. There's no real need for you to have the money you make at gambling. Come clean now. He's very fond of you and – this is only a guess – he probably already makes you a handsome allowance because you're the nearest kin he has . . . you're like a son to him. He dotes on you."

"Well? My God – you're a bit of a witch, aren't you?"

"No – I'm not. I'm a well-brought-up young lady – but I don't sit at home and sew a fine seam. I work – but I needn't. Mamma, like a lot of wealthy people, always cries poverty. It's like getting absolution before you can start sinning again and –"

"And I should think that was enough. My Goodness . . . I had no idea that such a beautiful creature was also a woman of such intelligence and good sense, and just the type I've always wanted. Sure, I'll come into all Uncle has some time – later than sooner I sincerely hope – but when I do I'll need help. What do you think? Should we get married now . . . or wait until . . . well things are a little more imminent?"

"I don't know what imminent means. But I'm not marrying anyone for a good while yet. That –" she suddenly smiled in an exaggerated and coquettish fashion – "Doesn't mean of course that I haven't got my eye on one or two people."

"Oh . . ." He took her by the arm, saying, "Let's go and dance a little while and you can tell me their names. I'll have arrangements made for them all to meet with accidents. And it's no good your grumbling about things . . . we're going to

157

get things properly fixed up. I only ask one thing about cards. I suppose you'd have no objection to neighbourly bridge at ten pence a hundred?''

"None at all."

He grinned. "Well, so long as this cruise lasts I must make the most of my freedom."

"You do that, my darling." She took his right hand, raised it to her mouth and bit his index finger gently, then gave a great sigh and said, "What a heavenly night . . . I'd no idea that anything so gorgeous and wonderful as this was going to happen. Mamma will be so excited and pleased. She thinks very highly of you, you know."

NINE

"Oh, I've got a touch of the Aphrodites and I am sure I am going to make a catch tonight." Suzie was admiring herself in the little travelling mirror she held in her hand.

Lily laughed. "Well you'd better do something soon or Aunt Rachel will never forgive me for not getting you married off on the cruise."

The two girls were stretching their sunbaked limbs on the bunks in their cabin before preparing themselves for drinks before dinner. They had spent a long and lazy day swimming, sunbathing, playing quoits and tennis and completing the afternoon pursuits with the luxury of having their hair done at one of the ship's salons. The conversation had drifted on to the past events of the cruise and in particular to the visit to the island of Cyprus which they both had particularly enjoyed. The vineyards and the fertile fields surrounding Limassol, the Troodos mountains rising beyond with their forests and quiet villages, the winter ski-runs they had seen in the distance. A quick visit had been arranged to the Kolossi Castle, once a Commandery of the Knights of St John, Curium. An hour or so had been spent shopping and admiring the fine Greek and Turkish handicrafts but the highlight of the day had been the lazing and picnicking on the Aphrodite Beach. They both contentedly complained of the burning sunscorched skin they suffered as a result of swimming and diving in the clear blue water. Suzie, who had never held her head under water for more than a second before (and then in the bath at home), had wondered at herself, snorkel-diving under John

Christopher's instructions to see the wonders of the rainbow-coloured fish. He seemed to know the names of all the fish which could be found in the sea around Cyprus and had amused her with names like Red Soldier fish, Amber Jack, Spotted Weaver, Stargazeer Butterfly Blenny and Painted Comber. She'd decided to check at the library when she got home to see if he was pulling her leg. The sea was so calm and buoyant that no skill seemed to be necessary.

"What on earth did Aphrodite want to come up out of the sea for when it is so beautiful down there on the bottom?" questioned Suzie, who was a little hazy about the story of this Goddess of Love.

"Well that will be something for you to read about when you get home. You'll have to get a book on Greek Mythology." Lily laughed, "I know one thing, I shall never again bathe in the sea around our country. I'd freeze, even in the middle of summer."

Suzie sighed in contentment, "I'm going to ring for a tray of tea before I have my bath. Isn't this a great life? I'd like it never to end. I shall always be eternally grateful to you, Lil, for thinking of me as your companion. And the clothes we were able to buy as well, they really have made me feel like something out of a film."

"Yes, I'm not sure that I want to go back to the old life again but let's not think about that yet awhile."

"Lily," Suzie questioned, "Tell me to mind my own business if you like, but I wondered . . . How are you and Richard hitting it off? I mean, do you think he's serious? I know he seems to be very keen on you but is it just a ship's romance?"

"Well, only time will tell," replied Lily guardedly before she was interrupted by the arrival of the steward with the tea and pastries. The girls set to on the goodies with healthy appetites and forgot to finish the conversation before changing for dinner.

*　　*　　*　　*

Richard Linton, handsome, suntanned and immaculate in cream tuxedo and black tie, joined the girls in the lounge bar.

"Now, my golden beauties," he said, "what are you drinking?"

"Well mine is tomato juice with a touch of Worcester sauce," replied Lily. "We shall be drinking wine at dinner and there is a long evening ahead of us."

He turned to Suzie, thinking that if he hadn't already fallen head over heels in love with Lily, who was glowing in a cerise wild silk, off the shoulder cocktail dress, her slim brown legs enhanced by delicately strapped gold sandals, he would surely be taken in by this sun blonde apparition in smart black figure-hugging apparel, which was apparently a hitherto nonedescript Suzie. "And your's, Suzie?"

"Well, as I intend to make this evening the highlight of my cruise, I'll settle for a beginning with gin and Italian, a touch of lemon . . . Oh, with ice, how's that?"

He laughed, "Well, as you say, it'll do for a start but I don't advise too many of those during the evening."

John Eggerton had managed to have the day away from his duties to be with his sister Margery and, with the special permission of the ship's captain on compassionate grounds, was to join the party at table number seven for dinner. He spotted the girls with Richard and beckoned them to join the little gathering drinking together at the glass-topped table in the corner of the lounge. Gradually the rest of the party extracted themselves from the other passengers and joined them. The last person from table number seven to come into the lounge was John Christopher, looking more conventional than usual in a cool cream linen suit. His skin had turned to light honey colour with the sea air and sun and it struck Suzie that he was a very attractive fellow. The gin and Italian was beginning to have an effect on her judgement; her head began to swim a little: she felt good, confident, cheeky and provocative. "John," she said, "we're sitting together at dinner. I reckon we'll look good together, you

161

know, me in black and you in your smart get-up, just like the couples on the coloured brochures. What do you think?"

John Christopher smiled and gave a little mock bow, "Charmed, I'm sure, it will be my great pleasure."

"Then that's settled," said Suzie as she took his hand and pulled him gently down into the chair next to her, where they continued their conversation.

Lily looked at Richard and winked, "Oh, Oh, I hope he isn't going to be the subject of her Aphrodites." Richard looked puzzled. "Don't worry, I'll explain later," she promised: "but this should be fun to watch."

Just then a young ship's officer approached John Eggerton with a message for him to go to the radio room. Margery was bitterly disappointed, for she immediately thought this meant he was called back to duty and she had so looked forward to the opportunity of having his company for the evening. However, he returned as the group were filtering into the dining-room, looking very serious. He drew her aside and though it would have been hard for her to analyse her reasons for knowing, she was at once aware that something out of the ordinary had happened and without need for thought, she said, "What's happened?" He was silent for a moment or two, a period of briefness which she sensed at once was, if only fractionally longer than normal, reflecting some reluctance or deep disturbance inhibiting his need to speak.

"John . . . What is it?"

He moved to her, took her right hand and held it, and then said, "About ten minutes ago the radio office had a call asking if I could make myself available to take a telephone call –"

"John . . . Whatever for? Oh . . . something's happened . . . something –"

"Now – don't rush things." He stepped forward and put his arm around her shoulders and held her close to him. "I took the call a little while ago. It was about Richard and from

162

your doctor. Richard's had a stroke and has been taken to hospital –"

"Oh, my God . . . Oh, I must –"

"Now, hold on. He said it would be a few days before they could assess the extent of the stroke and get some idea of the recovery prospects, though – and I know you would want the full truth – he said he doubted whether there could ever be an absolutely complete recovery. He would hopefully be able to live a normal life but there was bound to be some element of disability which couldn't be immediately assessed."

"Oh, Lord – I must get to him. And here I am right out in the middle –"

"Hold on. The doctor said that at the moment there was nothing anyone could do which wasn't already being done. But he agreed that as soon as it was possible you should go home and be with him."

"But how can I do that?"

"Well . . . it's not all that bad. We get into Haifa early in the morning. You can fly back from there. There's no other way, my love. But listen – if you want me to . . . well then, I'll get leave and come back with you."

"Certainly not. There would be nothing you could do. There's no earthly reason why you should come. No, I'll fly back and you carry on with the cruise. Did the doctor give you any details of the stroke?"

"Well, not a lot. Apparently he was at a Masonic dinner . . . fortunately there were two doctors there and they hustled him into hospital right away. Now . . . I know it's silly to say it . . . but just keep calm and try not to fuss too much." He stepped back from her and eyed her for a moment or two and then went on, "Things don't always work out the way we would like. And I don't know whether I should say this . . . but perhaps now when he has a real need for you, and only for you . . . then who knows? There may come into being a new kind of happiness between you."

Margery Chambers stared at herself in one of the large fitted wall mirrors over the table. Despite all her troubles she

163

had looked after herself. Not so far distant from the face she saw in the mirror she could fancy she saw the face which had looked at her from her mirror when as a young woman she had sat and made up before going off to meet Richard . . . He had always led, dominated her . . . but had been her lover, her man and was still her husband. *In sickness and in health* . . . She remembered the April day of their wedding. Daffodils and the hedges abandoning winter starkness before the first fresh green of bursting buds . . . and even inside the church the song of a blackbird in the churchyard yews coming clear and pure through an open window . . . *I take thee, Richard, to my wedded husband . . . for better, for worse . . . to love cherish and to obey till death* . . . Through the porthole over her brother's shoulder she saw the slow run and surge of the sea, sunlit with a bright orange evening sunset.

Her mind made up, she said firmly, "I shall fly back from Haifa in the morning if that is possible. Could you arrange that for me, John?"

"Yes, of course. The people here on the ship will radio the airport and get it all fixed up. But I think I ought to come with you."

"No. I know you would. But you could do nothing. You stay here at your job and join me after the cruise. There's one thing you can do for me, though."

"Yes."

"Don't say anything to any of the people at our table about my going. You can give them all the facts after I've gone. But not while I'm aboard. I just don't want any of them to know . . . I don't want to talk about it to anyone."

"All right." Then with a sudden grunt and shake of his head, he said, "I know you've got to go and you are right to go – but after the way he has treated you for years . . . It just makes me see red."

"But not for long. Maybe this will change everything."

"Oh, I'm sure it will," he said bitterly. "He might need you now, to push him about in a wheelchair, to feed him like a ch –"

164

"John!"

Tight-lipped, silent now, he met her gaze squarely and there was a silence between them. Then a faint smile moved on his face and he moved forward, saying "I've often thought it, and now I am certain of it. God gave to women a gift which he only gives to a few men from time to time – the gift of knowing and honouring true love and true forgiveness."

"Yes . . . but . . . but not a man's strength . . . inside . . . inside here." She beat her breast and then moved into his arms and began to weep, and he held her, cradled her to him and made word noises and comforting sounds while at the back of his mind a cold hard voice was repeating, "If it were me I'd let him rot . . . rot to rot, the rotten swine . . ." Instead he said gently, "Come, you must eat if you can and if we don't join the others for dinner there will surely be questions. We can talk quietly afterwards and then if you decide to fly home, I will get the lads to arrange a booking on a flight from Haifa airport in the morning."

As they took the vacant seats reserved for them at table number seven, they heard the rest of the party discussing the day tour of the Holy Land and in particular a visit to Jerusalem, due to take place the following day. Details had been posted on the information board and bookings for the trip had to be made after the meal.

The ship was at that moment easing its way into the port of Haifa and the momentum of the engines was slowly quietening, giving the promise of a peaceful evening and undisturbed sleep that night. It meant an early morning start for the tourists going ashore since there was so much to see and so much ground to cover.

"I'm sorry I wouldn't be able to accompany you anyway," John Eggerton replied to the enquiry as to whether he would be able to go on the tour. "Normally I would be on duty, as you know, but as it happens, Margery and I will be coming ashore because we have some urgent business to attend to in Haifa, so that cuts her out – she will be most disappointed to miss Jerusalem, won't you my dear?" His sister nodded, thankful that he had taken over the conversation for her and though those present were curious at her pallor and disinterest, they put it down to probable disorder or 'a touch of the sun'.

The colonel had obviously undertaken the organization of the bookings for their party. "That's Gloria and James – You my dear," to Mrs Picton, "Mrs Bell and the Captain, Richard? Yes? – and no doubt Lily and Suzie, we can't leave the young people behind, can we, what?"

"Oh, yes, we shall be there." Lily looked for confirmation at Suzie ploughing her way through Poached Fillet of Lemon Sole Créole, after a very substantial appetizer. "Um" . . . grunted Suzie both in appreciation of the food before her and in assent to the trip.

"That's it then," said the colonel. "I'll get the booking in right away after the meal. Don't forget, then: early breakfast. We don't want to miss the embarkation to the quayside."

"Wait a minute," called Mrs Bell from the far end of the table, "You haven't got John Christopher's name down. You'll be joining us as usual, John, won't you?"

There was an uncanny silence before John Christopher replied, so much so that the clatter and conversation of the tables in the dining room seemed to cease as he rose politely to reply to Mrs Bell.

"I am terribly sorry, I shall not be with you on your journey to Jerusalem tomorrow."

"But you must come," protested Lily. "We can't do without you, I mean we are so used to having you with us, you always seem to be guiding us in some way. Oh dear, I can't explain quite what I mean."

"I know exactly what you are trying to say Lily but the fact remains that I cannot be with you in the Holy City."

Suzie had awakened to the general feeling of disappointment around the table. She could not believe what she had heard. John Christopher not coming to Jerusalem. That didn't fit in with her plans at all. Besides it was like Lily had said, they couldn't do without him now. It seemed he was

166

part of them, they liked him – no, it was more than that – they loved him. . . . Oh dear, what was she saying? This must be the wine talking. "But John Christopher," she said, "why aren't you coming with us to Jerusalem?"

"It's quite a simple explanation," he replied calmly, "You see, I've been there before!"

*   *   *   *

The evening was not turning out to be what Suzie had planned. She had left the dining-room steadying herself from the effects of the wine, on the arm of her 'victim' John Christopher. Lily crossed her fingers and mentally put her friend's fate in the hand of God, a contradiction of safeguards she had to admit. James Goodbody was intrigued and amused at the little charade which was being enacted and he broadly winked at Suzie as she passed him. John had readily agreed to walk her around the upper deck. There was a cool breeze blowing across the water and little candytufts of cloudlets were scurrying across a full moon and away to join each other on a low bank on the horizon. The wind played with the soft loose curls on Suzie's brow and cooled the burning cheeks of the excited girl's face. So far so good, thought Suzie; but she was getting nowhere fast. Here was the moon, here was the girl and here was the boy – there were words of a song like that, she thought, but she couldn't put them together properly or remember the tune or she might have hummed it to see John's reaction. She decided to plunge straight in. It was now or never, she thought: so here goes.

"It's a heavenly night, John." She leaned comfortably on him. "Have you ever thought about marriage? Or perhaps you've already been married – divorced perhaps? You don't say much about yourself. We haven't a clue where you came from or where you are going. Mind you, it's none of our business. I wouldn't think you were attached, or what are you doing here by yourself? Maybe you're just looking

167

around. If you are," she said half jokingly, "I'm available. I'd take you without any questions asked – and I'd love honour and obey – without any objections to the wording of the promise at all."

John stopped and leaning on the rails of the deck, looked out at the sea. The stillness and the quiet of the engines permeated a peace and calm which seemed unusual. "Marriages, dear Suzie, are made in heaven and my name doesn't come under the category of 'Man and Wife' in the big book up there. I think, had it been so, then you would have most probably been on my selection list." He gave her a merry smile. "Are you so sure that *your* name is written under that heading?"

"Well, John," she replied seriously, "I'm a woman, not bad looking most people seem to think. I can certainly cook and look after a house and I've plenty of experience with controlling a crowd of boys. So if I'm not there, what other qualifications are needed?"

"Martha!" he mused.

"What are you talking about? I could have sworn you called me Martha."

"Suzie," he ignored her question, "Have you ever thought of doing anything else, other than eventually marrying and running a home of your own?"

"Oh, yes! Dress designer, model, air hostess, stewardess – you name it, I've thought of it. But what chance have I ever had of training for any of these careers? I did once think I would like to teach, but that was when I was a small child. You see, I lost my mother when I was six and father couldn't cope with looking after my brothers and me by himself. Because I was a girl, he put me in a convent school, you know Anglo-Catholic – very high Church of England. There were about twenty of us who boarded. I don't think he paid any fees, or very little – it must have been financed by the Church – but we were well looked after, and happy too. I remember we wore old fashioned pink-and-white gingham frocks and beautifully laundered white aprons trimmed with frills of broderie lace. Oh, I must be boring you, but you did ask."

"No, I'm not bored. Do go on," he said kindly.

"I remember the thick black woollen stockings we wore in winter – I hated them – but the nuns were nice. Sisters, we called them. My favourite was Sister Katherine. I had to draw a toadstool in an art lesson once and because she thought I had done well, as a reward she drew an elf sitting on it and she coloured it in and I've never forgotten it. They were teachers you see, well some of them. Some did the laundry and the cooking in the convent and they helped with the gardening and they kept silkworms on mulberry bushes. I can smell them now. I suppose they span the silk but I don't remember seeing that. I do remember the heavenly icecream they made and we could buy it with our pocket money. Raspberry, coffee and vanilla and I have never tasted anything like it since, it was super." Suzie did not know why she went on. John Christopher was listening intently and she didn't realize she was being more than usually talkative.

"Well, they taught me most of what I know, certainly how to cook and keep a house clean because we had to help. I can remember scrubbing the long kitchen tables and the floors. 'Always the way of the grain', the Sisters used to say. So you see they returned me to my father a regular little housewife but I longed to be a teacher. No, really, I wanted secretly to be a nun myself. We used to talk to the young girls who came into the convent in their outdoor clothes and waited to see them when they had changed into their simple habits. We were very envious. We attended the convent church when they took their novice's vows and received the right to wear white veils and finally when they took the holy vows and were married to God, then they wore black veils. It was very impressive.

"The nuns just said I was an impressionable young girl and I must live in the world outside first but I have often thought I would like to go back to that convent and be a nun and comfort and look after the little orphans there and teach them. Do you know, I really think I would still like to do that. My father and brothers are perfectly able to look after themselves now and I just love the thought of living in that old convent again. It's still there. Oh, dear, how I have rambled and what rubbish you must think I am talking!"

"Suzie, it's not rubbish. You have just unravelled your innermost longings. You've never had the chance or the opportunity before. If you marry a man, your life is not going to alter much. After a few years you will bear children and go through the whole process of mothering again but you have a 'Calling'. You have much more to offer God, worthy though that life would be. My advice to you is to think more about this. You're a lovely girl, Suzie, and even with your beautiful fair hair covered by a habit, you would make a lovely nun." He smiled mischievously. "I think you are under the heading 'Marriage to God' which is a sacred calling. Don't throw yourself away on the first man who will have you. Now I am going to take you back to your cabin, you will want to sleep, for you have a very early start in the morning. But before you go, Suzie, let me thank you for the wonderful gift you have offered me and say how much I appreciate being the one you honoured with the thought."

He kissed her lightly on the cheek and she felt filled with a lightness of spirit which had no comparison to the uplift she had got from the wine at dinner that night.

*　　*　　*　　*

Suzie stirred gently on her bunk but did not open her eyes when Lily came to bed. She had dropped off into a deep contented sleep and tried to think why she felt so free. No, it wasn't that – so sure. Yes, she knew exactly where she was going, what she was going to do with her life. She felt, well, rather like she had felt at home when she had finally decided what to cook for the boys' lunch. She liked making decisions and now she'd got to get organized, go to the convent, find

170

out how things were done, whether in fact they would accept her . . . but for the time being she was going to revel in this absolute luxury and she turned over thinking of the trip they were to make to Jerusalem the next day.

"You awake, Sue?"

"Um," she grunted, "half."

"Suzie, listen: I've got some news for you. Oh, wake up, love, I'm bursting to tell someone."

"You're engaged!" replied Suzie knowingly. She obligingly sat up in bed to get the full impact of what Lily was saying.

"Yes! How did you know? You witch!"

"Obvious, it was a sure thing you were going to be eventually. You've been on a moonlight deck with Richard and you have been listening to sloppy music all night. We saw you in the Neptune Room when we passed."

"Oh Suzie, I wanted you to be the first to know. I thought he'd wait to ask me properly until I visited them for the weekend. You know I told you I was going to, but somehow it all happened at once."

Lily had dropped down on to the side of Suzie's bunk and she threw her arms around the sleepy girl and said "Oh Sue, I'm so happy, nothing has ever happened to me like this before."

Suzie patted her on her bare shoulders. "Congratulations old girl. . . . I'm happy for you too. It's no more than you deserve. You'll make a good team and you will be a great help to Richard with the flowers and all that. Anyway, tell me all about it tomorrow. I want to go back to sleep or I'll never be able to get up in the morning."

"O.K. Suzie, but I wanted you to know. By the way, how did your evening go? The last time I saw you, you were riding on the moon!"

Suzie laughed, "Yes, but I got off and now I'm riding on a cloud."

"What do you mean? Oh I can tell something's happened. You didn't pull it off, did you? I mean, did you click with

John Christopher? I could tell you were going to try to seduce him in a manner of speaking. I never thought for one minute you'd manage it. Not him!"

Suzie turned over and pulled the bed linen around her head. From under the clothes she said, "No, I am going to be a nun!"

"Suzie! Now I know you're still sloshed!"

"It's true, Lil; if they'll have me I'm going to go back to the convent school where I was as a kid and I'm going to ask if they will help me to take vows. You see," she found herself giggling, "we are both going to be married – you to Richard and me to the Church."

The dumbfounded Lily undressed and got into bed. She had to let this news sink in. She knew Suzie well enough to recognize when she was being serious. She also knew that she had always thought Suzie would do something unusual to prove herself. What would Aunt Rachel say, about both of them for that matter? What would Sue's father and brothers say? Well, Suzie might change her mind yet but somehow she was sure she wouldn't.

"If you do, Suzie, what will your father and brothers do? How will they manage?"

"Not 'If I do'. I *shall* do and the boys will probably get married when I'm not around to look after them. High time too. And Dad, well, we'll have to cross that bridge when we come to it. We'll get your Aunt Rachel to keep an eye on him for me. Hey! Perhaps they'll get spliced! That would solve a lot of problems." Then letting out a big yawn, Suzie said "Nightie night, Lil, sweet dreams."

In a few moments the two sleeping girls were enveloped in the soft Mediterranean night, but not before Lily had thought and said out loud, "Funny how things are turning out on this cruise. I've got the feeling it's all to do with John Christopher's influence!"

172

TEN

No one saw John Christopher before they left in the ship's launches for the quayside of the Kishon Harbour in the port of Haifa. He hadn't appeared at breakfast but this was not unusual, since he often did not appear on deck until mid morning.

Margery Chambers, now neatly dressed for a journey, escorted by her brother John Eggerton in his ship's uniform, accompanied them on the small boat and the party were surprised to see that her luggage was being shipped with them. Now unable to keep the news to themselves any longer, Margery explained that she had had bad news from home, her husband had been taken ill and John was taking time off to put her on a flight to England from the Haifa airport. He would be returning to the ship and would continue his duties for the rest of the cruise.

The rest of the party, mainly those who shared table number seven in the dining-room, formed themselves into little groups, imparting and exchanging little bits of information and gossip which had come their way. All were exceedingly happy for Richard and Lily and it was agreed they should have a champagne celebration at some future time.

Gloria Picton and James Goodbody had joined the happy couple and were fast forming quite a close acquaintance. At dinner the previous night Richard and James had got into a conversation about politics and Richard had intrigued James talking about the complexities of Richard's father's career and finally his parliamentary election resulting in him becoming a Member of the House of Commons. Gloria, who had quite decided that her future lay with James but was determined that her life should not be spent following him around card tables and the roulette wheel, recognized that there was a strong element of chance in a political career. James had a good brain, he had a certain amount of influence in circles which would help him up the political ladder and he would eventually have enough money to enable him to live, whilst he nursed his constituency, should he be selected. The inherent gambler could be and would be harnessed and since Lady Luck usually followed him he should be successful.

Gloria was a member of the Conservative Association in her hometown and she knew enough about politics to be sure that the way up was not easy or quick. First she must introduce James into the Association. He must take an active part on branch committees, take an interest in social functions, get known and liked. That shouldn't be difficult. James was a popular chap and was used to meeting people. Maybe the best thing would be for him to stand for council. She knew that at local elections the Party was on the lookout for suitable candidates. He should apply to go on the parliamentary candidate's list, but not too quickly – perhaps get representation at executive level . . . area level . . . maybe national level. . . . It would all take time but she was prepared to help him. She could play the part – she had money to give him the back up until he got his inheritance, they both had the necessary education. It would take a long time but they had their life ahead of them and both were young enough, though not too young, to embark on this venture.

She'd spoken to James about this after dinner last night and he had quickly responded to the idea. Mother? Well it didn't seem that she would need Gloria to accompany her on any more cruises, in fact she'd probably be in the way and she had no intention to play 'gooseberry' to Mother and the Colonel, who had taken up the close attachment which had been dropped in their youth. Gloria could see their relationship developing each day and her mother was as good at planning her future as she herself was. Like mother like daughter she thought.

Mrs Nancy Bell and Captain Langton had taken Suzie under their wing. They had both noticed the girl was thoughtful and quiet since the happy Lily was so taken up with her Richard; they felt Suzie was in need of companionship.

A coach met them on the quayside and they were taken to the main residential and shopping area of Haifa and so on to Mount Carmel where, from some three hundred metres above the town, they had a magnificent view of the beauty of the area. To the north and inland of the Carmel range lay the plain of Esdraelon or Megiddo, scene of one of General Allenby's victories over the Turkish army in 1918. On the slopes of Mount Carmel they saw the golden-roofed shrine of the Bahai faith set in beautiful gardens and the guide pointed out the Gan-haem (Mothers Garden), a museum of prehistory, biological institute and zoo, the museum of ethnology and folklore and the great synagogue. In the distance, about ten miles out of the city, they were told, lay the colourful Druse villages and to the south the artists' village of Ein Hod. To the south-east lay the excavation of a second-century Jewish town and, in the same direction, the museum and excavation of the stables and bulwark of King Solomon.

Coffee had been arranged for them at the Hotel Dan Carmel before the coach took them along the south coast road, through Caesarea and the modern metropolis of Tel Aviv and so to Jerusalem. The main centre of the tour – Jerusalem – high in the hills to the south of Haifa – the lands of the Bible all around. They climbed the stony steps of the Mount of Olives. Suzie shivered as a cool breeze made her put her cardigan on. The trees were leaning and slightly stunted by the wind and the grass was sparse and bare and she felt lonely and sad and a bit frightened, even though

175

there were others from the party around her and the guide was still incessantly talking and pointing out the panoramic view of the walled city of Jerusalem dominated by the golden Dome of the Rock.

Suzie pulled herself together and followed the others, who were now descending to the Garden of Gethsemane where Jesus was betrayed by Judas. A nice walled garden with gnarled olive trees. Could they have been here in Christ's time? They looked so old and time worn. She'd have to ask Lily, she'd know how long they could survive. The sun was warm and the garden was sheltered. and Suzie could understand the disciples falling asleep on the warm sandy soil, with the wall protecting them from the cool breeze of the hilltops. Next they visited the Western Wall and wondered at the informality of the chairs at its foot and the tables covered with dark gold-fringed cloths on which lay books of Jewish law. From these tables, the guide explained, rabbis would conduct the ceremony of the bar-mitzvah, when young Jewish boys at the age of thirteen years recited long passages conscientiously learnt for this purpose.

They looked up at the majesty of the great stature of this historic wall, lichen invaded and stacked with huge stone blocks of different shapes and sizes, defying age and time.

"This is the most holy place for the Jews," the guide explained. "After lunch we shall continue our conducted walk in the ancient walled city passing through the Temple area. We shall see the Dome of the Rock revered by the Moslems. Here the Bible comes startlingly alive, but before we begin our walk up the Via Dolorosa, the Way of Sorrows, along which our Lord carried his cross on the last agonizing journey, I suggest we split up for an hour and you can take advantage of seeing the shops and bazaars and having a spot of lunch."

"We're going to Plaza Sheraton. It's central and handy and you can get lunch on the Summer Terrace," Mrs Picton announced as the party dispersed, "Anyone joining us?"

Lily and Richard had decided to find a pavement café

176

where they could sample the traditional food of the Israelis. Mrs Bell and the Captain declined the invitation on the grounds that they wanted to explore the bazaars a bit before finding a place for a quick snack. Suzie wanted to do some shopping and decided only to pop in somewhere to eat if she had the time and the inclination. Gloria and James hailed a taxi and drove off with Mrs Picton and the Colonel, while the rest of their small party walked through the maze of narrow alleys, intrigued by the colourful bazaars and inhaling the smell of the spicy food and the tempting fish dishes of the traditional eating houses.

The newly engaged couple found a pavement café of their choice and were enjoying the shade which the bright awning was giving from the sun while they tucked in to the meal of *fallafal*, a popular dish of pastry, meat and onion filling accompanied by new rolls and followed by fresh fruit. Waiting for coffee to be served, Lily watched Suzie, who hadn't moved far away from them, as she turned over the materials on one of the stalls and a vendor tried to persuade her to buy. "He'll never get over that one," she said to Richard. "She's much too fly."

It was an unforgettable scene, the black shadows of the archways contrasting with the whiteness of the sunscorched buildings. A mixture of races thronged the streets, Arabs, Moslems, Jews, Europeans and many others. Lazily Lily watched Mrs Bell and Captain Langton as they browsed. Smiling she watched them disappear into a shop full of antiquities. "He's a funny chap, that Captain Langton," she said to Richard. "Mrs Bell seems so fond of him but I think he brags an awful lot about the things he has done and, do you know, I think they are all fibs. I can't think what she sees in him."

"It takes all sorts to make a world," replied Richard. "Look at this scene for instance – did you ever see such a mixture of humanity? Take that for instance." He pointed into the street. "He looks just as if he had stepped out of a Bible story."

177

Lily saw an old man wearing long, loose robes, the cloth covering his head held in place with a ring of twisted cotton. He was leading a donkey carrying goods in a pannier on each side of its body. It took no notice of the dodging traffic of bicycles, taxis, buses and people crossing from side to side. It walked slowly and steadily along the twisting road, so slowly that a small child who had been playing under the tables of one of the bazaar holders, ran out and, seeing no danger, crossed the road. She reached the middle but not in time to get across in front of the donkey. She hesitated, then, thinking to wait until the beast had passed, ran backwards into the way of an oncoming taxi.

The screech of brakes and the screams attracted Suzie's attention to the scene and before she could ascertain what was happening she saw Captain Langton throw himself on the child, flinging her out of the way of the taxi. She heard the dull heavy thud of the Captain's body as the taxi struck him down. As in a nightmare she saw Richard and Lily leaning over the man lying in the street and the ashen face of Mrs Bell as she sank into the arms of a passer-by and fainted at the sight of her companion's lifeless body.

*   *   *   *

A very sorry party returned in the coach along the motorway to Haifa late that afternoon, without Mrs Bell and the Captain. It was fortunate that the Colonel had returned to the scene of the accident in time to take things in hand. The Captain was still breathing but they were told he had no chance of survival. His heartbroken Nancy had accompanied him to hospital and refused to leave until he had drawn his last breath.

"You know, Lil," Suzie told her friend later. "While we were at the hospital with her, she told me they had gone into that shop to buy a ring. She showed it to me. It wasn't much, you know, the sort of thing tourists buy in the bazaars – kind of engraved gold band and a biblical motif in the place of a stone – pretty though – sort of gold and blue enamel. It was a setting sun with all the rays coming out from the centre and against them was a white dove with outstretched wings. Mrs Bell said that, for a joke, the Captain put it on her finger, the middle one of the left hand – then he became serious and he altered it and put it on her engagement finger and then asked her to marry him and she accepted. Then she said a funny thing, she said: 'I was so happy that he decided to give me the chance to have him for what he really was and not for the things he thought he ought to have done!' Then she said, 'If only he knew that the last thing he would do was the bravest of them all.' "

*   *   *   *

It was late when they boarded the SS *Andreas* again. No one felt like eating and the party dispersed to their respective berths.

Lily and Suzie were very quiet, neither wishing to relive the events of the accident, but it was impossible to avoid the thoughts which were uppermost in their minds. Thoughtfully, Suzie said, "I'm going along to find John Christopher, he probably hasn't been told about the Captain's accident yet." Without waiting for any answer, Suzie made her way to cabin number seven. She didn't know what motivated her, for she had never been to the cabin before but she knew the way without asking anyone. When she arrived the door was a little ajar. She knocked but there was no answer. Pushing open the door gently, she looked inside. The cabin was empty. Suzie didn't know what she had expected to find but somehow she thought John Christopher would have been there inside the cabin, lying on his bunk, reading or something. The cabin was empty. She couldn't think why this made such an impression on her. Something told her it was no use looking for him anywhere else. She opened the wardrobe. No clothes – no luggage – no personal things on tables and chests. The late pink and purple rays of the sinking sun streamed through the portholes and the softened light fell on a small pile of cream linen lying on the bed – the clothes he had worn last night, the last time she saw him. She was puzzled.

A slight movement behind her made her turn to see someone standing there. "Who are you?" she asked.

"Don't you recognize me, Suzie?" the man replied.

"Where is John Christopher?" she asked.

"He's gone – he's disembarked – didn't you know? He only took a one-way ticket, you know."

Suzie sank down on the chair by the door to collect her thoughts and then she looked up to thank the steward for his information but he had disappeared.